lesley howarth

ultraviolet

PUFFIN BOOKS

For my father
Donald Edward Howarth
1916–1999

PUFFIN BOOKS

Published by the Penguin Group
Penguin Books Ltd, 27 Wrights Lane, London W8 5TZ, England
Penguin Putnam Inc., 375 Hudson Street, New York, New York 10014, USA
Penguin Books Australia Ltd, Ringwood, Victoria, Australia
Penguin Books Canada Ltd, 10 Alcorn Avenue, Toronto, Ontario, Canada M4V 3B2
Penguin Books India (P) Ltd, 11 Community Centre, Panchsheel Park, New Delhi – 110 017, India
Penguin Books (NZ) Ltd, Cnr Rosedale and Airborne Roads, Albany, Auckland, New Zealand
Penguin Books (South Africa) (Pty) Ltd, 5 Watkins Street, Denver Ext 4, Johannesburg 2094,
South Africa

On the World Wide Web at: www.penguin.com

Penguin Books Ltd, Registered Offices: Harmondsworth, Middlesex, England

First published 2001
1

Copyright © Lesley Howarth, 2001
All rights reserved

The moral right of the author has been asserted

Set in Joanna MT

Made and printed in England by Clays Ltd, St Ives plc

Except in the United States of America, this book is sold subject to the condition that it shall
not, by way of trade or otherwise, be lent, re-sold, hired out, or otherwise circulated without
the publisher's prior consent in any form of binding or cover other than that in which it is
published and without a similar condition including
this condition being imposed on the subsequent purchaser

British Library Cataloguing in Publication Data
A CIP catalogue record for this book is available from the British Library

ISBN 0–141–31078–2

Contents

Contents

Chapter 1

Cyber Spring————

Imagine you never went to school. Never went out with your friends. Stayed home and studied on the computer. Not now and then. All the time. You have a best friend named Reeve. You see her whenever you can. Other friends, maybe you e-mail or 'meet' in guestrooms in games like the Quest. A night out? Forget it. Everyone forgot how to 'do' friends, now no one goes out any more.

Violet Niles drags her eyes from her double in the mirror and takes a pair of dressmaking scissors to a gleaming sheet of blue plastic. But soon her eyes wander back. *Want to know what I look like? Take a look in the mirror. Ultra-me, ultra-you. Where I am now, you could be in twenty years' time. Looking backwards, it happened so quickly. How were we to know the sun would just burn up our lives?*

The scissors rip cleanly around the shapes laid out on the sheet of blue plastic covering the floor. The arms and the hood and the back of what looks like a jacket are already cut out, when someone comes up through the tunnel. Visitors are so unusual that Violet Niles has to compose her face before she can meet them. She puts down her scissors reluctantly. The chances that Nick has heard them are pretty remote.

Outside the window the sun burns down, a giant nuclear cooker converting hydrogen to helium. Core temperature, 15.6 million Kelvin. Core pressure, 250 billion atmospheres. Energy, output at 36 billion billion megawatts, is produced by nuclear fission. In the giant exchange from hydrogen to helium, energy is carelessly thrown off.

Every kind of radiation, that's what the sun throws off, right on to the unprotected head of the little town of Condorcet. Every year more and more ozone-eating clouds appear on the skyline each spring. Now the winter solstice, 21st December, marks the beginning of the only two or three months it's safe to go outside. Other than that, the tunnels reach out, tunnels between lonely compounds like the one surrounding Violet Niles' home. Someone coming, now; feet approaching like a drum – boom – boom – ker-boom.

The tunnels gleam like a black spider on the desert under dangerous ultraviolet-B radiation beaming in from a cloudless blue sky. Inside the black spider the long, ribbed tunnels have a life of their own. Conversations and door closures wafted on the air conditioning produce strange quacks and clashes, whispers, booms, sudden shouts, howls and prophesies.

You want to see into the future? Vi smells the tunnels already. Her eyes meet the mirror again. *Look at what's happening now. Sun getting a little hotter each year? You think it won't affect you?*

Look at those groaning supermarket shelves, and ask yourself, how can this last?

Boom! Boom! Blit-blat!

Violet! Answer the tunnel! Scolding herself into it, Vi descends the stairs, the sickly tunnel-niff from the burping flap in the kitchen wafting over her in the hall.

'Hey.' The tunnel-flap closes behind the second of them, a boy with a rubber neck. The first boy carries a box. Her two visitors blink under the lights of the kitchen waking up around them. Smart walls offer a games menu or current television news.

'Hey.' Roddy and Jope. Now then.

'Slides for the doc. My dad to yours.' Roddy extends a box marked 'Niles'.

Eye-contact, it's important. Vi smiles and takes it. 'Not coming to see me then?'

'No,' Roddy says truthfully.

Vi shelves the box. 'Anything else?'

'That's it.'

'I just wondered.'

'Right.'

Roddy's dad works at the Uni. Roddy and Jope hang out. Slides or files often come with Nick's B12 shots or a multi-pack of Vit. D, since the Jopes run Condorcet Druggist.

'Big garden,' Danny Jope tells his feet. 'How much does your old man make?'

'He's working for BluShield.'

'On telly?'

'As an ultraviolet consultant.'

Jope whistles. 'Brisk.'

'Grow many strawberries?' Roddy hopes.

'Like some?'

'You serious?'

'Remind me,' Vi promises lightly. Soft fruits almost never crop up at the co-operative food stations, where potatoes are a priority. 'They're not that great. Really.'

'Gardens, so what?' Jope tells Roddy. 'Strawberries blow. I told you.'

They don't blow but raspberries are better, Vi wants to say, but doesn't, not wanting to rub it in, aware that she and her father, Nick, take luxuries like strawberries for granted.

Only people like Doctor Nick Niles can afford a Shielded garden. Berries and squash, peppers and beans, these are the marks of success. Protected from too much ultraviolet radiation by shining sheets of BluScreen, made exclusively by BluShield Worldwide, vegetables can germinate, while plants outside under a hundred per cent increase of UV-B fail to grow at all. Plus there's no risk of sunburn yourself, while you're out under the Blu thinning carrots. Rusting Ferrari in the driveway? Forget it. Lettuces say 'I Made It', broccoli, 'I'm a Star.'

And Doctor Niles is a star. The Friendly Face of Science, wheeled out every spring to reassure everyone, everywhere, that Technology Has The Solution to survival under ultraviolet-B, now stunting crops everywhere. Tardigrades are his speciality. But nobody knows what they are.

'Better go now,' Roddy says.

'Not yet.' Vi gropes for welcoming words. 'Might as well Quest, now you're here.'

They troop upstairs to her bedroom and stand around at a loss.

'Take a seat.'

They take one.

'Like a drink?'

'Why not?'

Vi fetches three glasses of cranberry juice. 'Know what tardigrades are?'

Jope shrugs. Sips his juice.

'Microscopic animals living in water droplets. They're called the Bears of the Moss. Nowhere damp on the planet you can sit down without scraping up a population or two under your fingernails. Dad says –' Vi takes a slug of juice; wipes her mouth in a gesture unconsciously like Nick's – 'Dad says if the eco-system breaks down, cockroaches, tardigrades and BluShield executives will be the only survivors.'

Jope's cranberry-juice smile doesn't flicker. Nick's joke isn't funny at all, now she brought it out in the open.

Roddy drains his glass. 'Anything to eat?'

'Brown rice.'

Roddy gags.

'Remember,' Danny Jope says, 'when the supermarkets were filled with food?'

Roddy nods slowly. 'Millions of different kinds of everything.'

Millions of different kinds of everything. But how quickly

had it all gone, evaporated away, like a puddle under the sun, and *Vi had seen it would happen!* This first vision hadn't been easy to understand. At the age of four, Vi had been standing in the supermarket with her mother when the food all around her melted – just melted away. The oven chips, pizzas, ice cream, pastry and peas simply disappeared inside the supermarket freezers as she looked at them. She blinked, looked again – everywhere, nothing – blinked again; back it came, for how long? Impossible to make her mother understand! Did she realize that all this was temporary?

From then on, Violet Niles repeatedly glimpsed the supermarket shelves *as they would be,* as empty of food as they were in other, less fortunate, parts of the world – and learned that no one else saw it. The over-stacked aisles made her cry – soon, soon, they would be gone. Mummy, buy more, buy more. The bulging freezers yawned empty and white as she looked at them. On the shelves she glimpsed a single loaf of bread; through the overfilled trollies a lonely can of beans.

Slowly at first, then quickly, everything she saw came true. Fresh produce disappeared over a summer when nothing much grew, and overdates canned veg replaced it. Then the slide to odd cans released from food mountains and shortages of green things was rapid. She could have said, 'I told you so.' Instead, she kept it to herself. But that didn't stop her from seeing things. More things, as she grew older. She wrote to an advice column about it. *I see things before they happen. I want to get rid of it.* The answer advised her to read books to develop her imagination in a more constructive way, the kind of reply she'd foreseen. Still she saw and said nothing, except to the bedroom mirror, sensing how weird it was, how far beyond the normal range, how ultra-Violet.

Ultraviolet radiation beyond the normal range was the reason fruit and vegetables, then milk and bread and meat, began to disappear. Now shopping at Wesley Food Cooperative is a matter of grabbing strange windfalls of oil or millet, canned faggots, compressed packs of dates, ancient rice pudding, dried chickpeas from some chickpea mountain, nobody knows how old. Distant memories of chocolate mini-rolls, crisps, bread rolls, cola, Tangle Twistas, grapes, yoghurts and Choco Pops, make the chickpeas worse. *Remember when the supermarkets were full of food?*

'And the birds,' Vi remembers, 'in spring.'

'Frozen chickens, you mean?'

'The birds,' Vi repeats. 'Outside.'

Roddy nods again, though he doesn't remember them at all. Outside in the garden the sunshine shimmers over the trees, but only the shyest of birds occasionally nest in them now. Only black cats slink out after them, and even they stick to the shadows. All the white cats live indoors and all the white birds died.

'Let's load *Lambkin*,' Jope suggests.

'Not the Quest?'

'After that.'

UltraViolet downloads from 'Freegame' and *Lambkin* fills the room with the long-forgotten sounds of spring.

Jumping lambs. Tweeting thrushes. It's as if they're walking into a meadow, as summer fields of green open before them over the wall.

'What *are* thrushes?' Jope asks.

'I know this.' Vi has to think pretty hard. 'They're brown – no, black.'

'Aren't they spotty or something?'

Plunging through banks of primrose, they zero in on a thrush. Its speckled breast swells with a song so ever-changing and inventive, it seems it'll never repeat itself or end its variations on the joyful note of spring.

'Wish spring was really like this,' Roddy says.

'Brisk colours,' Jope agrees, as *Lambkin* shows them the black velvet eye of a tulip. 'Should tulips be out with snowdrops?'

'You know about flowers, but not about birds?'

'Maybe I don't. So what?'

Tulips bloom in cyber spring whenever you want them to. Late-flowering summer roses at the same time as bluebells? No problem. You can 'grow' spring any way you like. *Lambkin* is all about colour and movement. The meadow falls behind them as Vi steps up the speed. A blazing field of daffodils beckons them into a valley where hawks clash overhead. The sounds are supra-real, the colours pulsating; only the scents are missing, and the feel of a summer breeze.

Jope says, 'Add some rabbits – what's this?'

He wrenches out plastic from under him. Vi takes it off him and quickly folds it away.

Jope looks at her.

Vi looks back. 'I'm making a suit. What?'

'Of BluScreen?'

'Why not?'

'For?'

'Going outside.'

'Not until Solly.'

'Yes.'

'No.'

'You can't, you know,' Roddy says seriously.

'Why not, if I'm Protected?'

'No one goes out till Solstice Day. You Know It Makes Sense,' Jope adds.

'It's a good suit. It'll protect me.'

Colours flash. Hawks dive. Supra-real blossoms open.

'Everyone will be wearing them soon. That's the way it'll go – Protective suits for everyone.'

Violet Niles' premonitions have a way of coming true. Roddy and Jope bring up their guns, raking the fields of Lambkin for scudding rabbits, racking up scores over the three-hundred mark each and entering them in Overachievers Top Scores.

'Where did you get the BluScreen?' Jope asks casually.

'Old stocks in the garage.'

'Let's see.'

They troop downstairs to the garage under the house. Vi unlocks the door reluctantly.

'Not supposed to go in here.' It feels like a betrayal.

And there they are. Three hefty rolls of prototype Blu,

from the time Nick first worked as a consultant for BluShield Worldwide.

Jope whistles. 'Know how much these are worth?'

'Not allowed to sell it, so it doesn't matter anyway.'

'Sell some to me.' Jope feels the width.

'Doesn't the old man mind you cutting it up?' Roddy retrieves some slivers of Blu from the floor.

'I'll sell it on. Give you a cut,' Jope persists.

'Can't do that.'

'Why not? He'll never know.'

UltraVi pushes Jope out of the garage. Shuts the house-door and locks it. 'Forget I showed you, all right?'

Jope's face seems to say, What's it worth? But this could be game paranoia. They troop back upstairs and load the Quest, but somehow the mood is shattered and Vi wishes they'd go. They surprised her over the garage. She shouldn't have taken them down there. Nick wouldn't have liked it, and the thought of it doesn't feel good. She goes over things she might have said to put them off, as the thudding opening bars of the monstrous overture of *QuestHolme* thunder around the room.

Enough with games like *Lambkin* already.

'Switch to immersive,' Jope says.

Three people in headsets sit on Violet Niles's bedroom floor. A fly persistently buzzes the glass of juice beside Roddy's hand. Meanwhile, the action in Usher Wood, a level of *QuestHolme Gothic*, runs silently over the walls. Since no one killed 'Wall Display', it mirrors the virtual action experienced by the three figures now swaying in synch, strangely like flies themselves in their bulging black VR headsets. Vi has a feelie — a soft-toy dog. It should crop up in her gameplan, as she 'sees' the shape she feels.

The figures could be anywhere, instead of on the bedroom floor. Treated blinds over the windows block out any sign of light. Between the bed and the living walls, strips of a strong, blue plastic lie forgotten on the floor. Violet Niles, where's your determination to finish it? Your suit of Blu awaits you! And the world outside!

Outside the garden grows under its Protective dome. As growing plants reach up to touch it, a sensor causes the BluScreen to creep up its poles, so that the dome grows with them. Beyond it, the sun bakes cabbage leaves that have accidentally grown outside the Protected area.

Inside the bedroom the three figures sway. Roddy knocks over his juice. It wells around his buttocks, but he's living in QuestHolme now. The fly zeroes in on a pink finger of juice creeping across the carpet. Nick Niles grins out of a photograph on Vi's noticeboard. 'Accepting the Award of the Association of Ionospheric Sciences, 5 June, 2020,' the photograph is headed. Vi becomes aware of a sinking feeling, deep in Usher Wood. Either it's Usher Bog or —

Removing her headset, she jumps up. Something spilt somewhere. She fetches a cloth and cleans it up. Stupid idiots are sitting right in it. Oblivious to wet jeans, Roddy and Jope play on. The soft seams made around their bodies by the flooding pink juice stir an idea in UltraVi's mind.

Abandoning both them, taking up the pieces of BluScreen suit covering her bedroom floor, she retires to the adjoining workshop, where, late into the night, the smell of hot plastic lingers ...

How rude of her. She forgot to give her visitors their strawberries.

Seems like they didn't miss her. The only sound betraying the departure of Roddy and Jope is the *blit-blat* of the kitchen tunnel-flap as they eventually log off and leave.

Chapter 2

Tunnels & Taureans—

The girl with the violet eyes stands over the guard's body, grabbing frantically for his keys. Did the other guards hear his muffled scream? The dungeon drips. Rat scuffle. Silent Henchmen dart around nearby corners and may attack at any time. Deep in the belly of the dungeon, she has only a Questkey, her knowledge of martial arts and her wits to aid her escape. With ninety levels of hell to get through, she has to grab clues as she goes.

Some neat visual effects never before seen in *QuestHolme Two: Ravendale* take the girl with the violet eyes deep into a labyrinth under the dungeon, where three Henchmen surprise her. A swift turn sees the scimitar of the Emperor Seshwan whistle past her head. He skipped Editions – she didn't know he could do this. With a double back-flip, the girl with the violet eyes whips the next Questclue from around the evil Emperor's neck. Throwing Seshwan three times for luck, she opens a worm-hole with her remaining Health Score, escaping through five different levels. I *don't feel I need this*. The girl with the violet eyes strips off her headset wearily. Enough with Henchmen for now.

Immediately the action switches to the smart walls of her bedroom, lighting her face and clothes with *Ravendale* greens and blues. With relief she removes the interactive glove lined with infra-red sensors. Those Quest loops. Run them enough, they can mess with your mind and make you believe anything. At least with wall display you know where you are, though this level has her stumped.

With a few swift keystrokes on the computer beside her bed, she downloads the instructions for the latest edition of QuestHolme:

'Take any disguise you want,' the QuestGuide enthuses. *'Enter any scenario. With a "multiple path" feature as standard, many levels will have two exits, and different exits will lead to different levels. There are over twenty thousand ways to finish the scenario as a result! Thirty-six total levels, though you'll only see around twenty as you play through. Hundreds of thousands of fanatics have escaped the Quest at the dungeon — can you crack the clues and solve it?'*

QuestHolme Two: *Ravendale* really pushes the envelope. Those super-fast levels of clue-gathering under fire are going to wear down anyone's defences, no matter how brisk they are. Anyone escaping *Ravendale* to reach QuestHolme Three: *The Great Wall of China*, with health status and ammo intact, is going to be congratulating themselves on some pretty spectacular action.

Yet it's old, already.

Already the Quest has moved up a quadrillion dimensions in less than a year. Edition Seven lets you paste your world into the gameplan. After someone calling themselves 'Random Squires' customized Edition Six, the makers issued new QuestGuides. With pirated Editions popping up all over the place, you could paste in some pretty personalized scenarios with realistic 'home' backdrops, chisel or kick-box your folks, 'shoot down' anyone you wanted to. For a while the Quest got tainted with all the trouble. Studies showed that *Ravendale* could stimulate aggression. Other studies showed that failing to tie your shoelaces against the clock stimulated aggression.

Vi doesn't care about this too much. But she does miss Random Squires, who occasionally sent out new instructions himself about customized 3-D Editions. 'Random Squires' web site got wiped after legal trouble. No one can contact him now. The makers of *QuestHolme*, who sued him then tried to employ him, don't even know where he is. But he did force the game to develop with lightning speed. On any given day or night, almost eighty per cent of those under eighteen are going to be deep in the Quest.

'Make character?' the screen prompts.

'YES', options Violet Niles.

'Paste in …?'

'MILT.'

'Near end?'

'LEVEL FIFTY-TWO.'

'Wall display or Quit?'

It must be morning.

'QUIT.'

Even someone named Violet Niles isn't going to miss out on *QuestHolme*. And with the sun burning up the world outside, indoor opportunities for gameplaying knock almost every day, but still ... you have wash sometime ...

Who are you going to meet today? her reflection in the bathroom mirror asks her. *No one, if you don't go out,* it answers itself, pretty smartly.

Cleaning her teeth, Vi checks her tadpoles in the bath. The air in the bath is always cool and languid, no matter how jittery the air-conditioning gets. So it's a pain to lift the vivarium out, the odd time you feel like a bath. The vivarium only stays in the bath until the tadpoles grow 'arms'. Then they need to be released. Vi understands them now. These are the fifth crop she's raised, getting good at it at last.

Vi pads back to her room. The result of her night's work lies gleaming and complete on the bed. She Quested a little to reward herself. Now why not try it on? All it takes is a little courage. Today could be the day.

Raising the Treated blinds, it's possible to gauge the strength of the sun from the heat-shimmer over the black plastic tunnel cooking beneath her window. The tunnel makes its way from the back of the house, past the BluScreened garden, to a bunch of defeated-looking trees. Beyond them, at Locke Junction, domestic tunnels join the permanent tunnel to town, a thundering black plastic rat-run known as the Hobbes Boulevard.

The heat in domestic tunnels can reach surprising heights in summer. Visitors prepared to walk down them are almost a thing of the past. Once you could stroll into town. Now summers stretch into warm winters as too much ultraviolet radiation hits the earth in short and dangerous wavelengths. At the front of the house, once the path to town, the defeated trees hang on. Beyond the Hobbes Boulevard, the town of Condorcet sits like a spider on the desert. The tunnels connecting the compounds to town are rolled out earlier every spring. But now the old black plastic tunnels are cracking under too much UV-B.

No one has come up with replacement tunnels yet. And so the spider extends its legs every February, and the black plastic simmers outside. Old technology. For a sustainable future. And still the temperature climbs. So Vi Quests most of the day, and most of the timeless night, bloodying her mouth with cranberries in the garden whenever she remembers she's hungry. Sometimes she meets her father in the sweetcorn, or finds him out under the moon, thoughtfully eating a radish.

Some nights Nick cooks brown rice, then heads back upstairs to his studio. The sounds of *QuestHolme* thunder from Vi's room as he thoughtfully switches slides under the microscope and shoots his B12 vitamins into his bulging forearm. It doesn't even register with him which particular game fills the house, and most houses round it, beyond the compound. These problem-solving games stimulate the brain to produce more pathways. Can't have enough dendrites. God knows, he could use some more. His skin feels like it could crawl right off his back this morning. Lactic acid build-up from those tricep clenches, maybe.

Down to the kitchen. Open the blinds. A glaring sun outside. How about an antioxidant cocktail, lemme see, where's those melons –

'So what do you think?' Violet Niles emerges in her suit of Blu, like a gleaming chrysalis, into the kitchen.

Nick throws back a handful of vitamins. 'You Quest all night?'

'After I finished this.' She gives him a twirl.

'What time is it?'

'Nine-ten. You haven't said what you think.'

Nick selects a watermelon from a net over the breakfast bar. Squints at Vi over his shoulder. She cut the odd suit out of BluScreen before. But this time the seams are tight. 'The food-bag sealer in the workshop, right?'

'Heat-welded seams. Came to me last night.'

'Fine, if they don't bubble.'

'Why not make these for everyone?' Vi holds out her arms, entranced with the feeling of Protection. 'Make the neck big enough, you don't need a zipper. Hood was the difficult bit.'

'Dead in the water.' The doc disembowels the watermelon into the blender.

'Why?'

'Bad psychology.'

'How?'

'Okay, people don't like it. Kind of panics 'em to think they have to wear a suit to go outside. Easier to pretend they don't want to, and stay indoors.'

He has a point. The suit makes you feel like one of those

armoured tardigrades he has in diagram on the wall. *Pseudechiniscus*, particularly, with its red segmented backplate and lateral appendages, looks like it's going to war. A war, Vi thinks, against the worst that the sun can throw at us this year.

'Going out dressed like a moss-bear has to be safe, right?'

'Outside?'

'Why not?'

The doc hits a switch and the watermelon explodes in the blender. Removing the top, he throws back his head and gulps down the pink pulp, wipes his mouth with his hand, offers the jug to Vi. 'Antioxidant cocktail – seeds, flesh, the lot.'

'Dad. The suit.'

Nick Niles considers it. 'Want me to road-test it for you?'

'Simulated radiation, you mean?' Vi lifts the kitchen blind. 'It's only nine o'clock. I could test it now, outside.'

'Not on my time, you won't.' Nick reminds her he has a responsibility to her mother while she's staying with him. Like living with a science freak, in a house where time is meaningless, isn't going to mess with her mind.

UltraViolet has learned to invent her own life, since no one's about to do it for her. Her father leads a science-life. He led a drunk life before. He was wrecked the day he named her. Sent to register her as 'Rose', he called at a bar to toast her arrival. By the time he arrived at the Registry, he couldn't remember which flower. 'Lily' would have been better, but it could have been a lot worse. Now he shoots his vitamins, studies his blood for DNA mutations, cooks up a tub of brown rice every two or three days. Sometimes they might bump heads in the vegetable patch, cook up a hash of fresh veg together; then they might do deep-field blood work till morning, using samples taken from the delivery boy bringing a fresh 'scope lens up the tunnel.

Nick takes up a file headed 'International Tardigrade Statistics'.

'I'm e-mailing this month's Profiles. Ice-cream in the maker.'

Shedding the suit on the floor, Vi cracks open the ice-cream maker. Waving a spoon, thinking as she talks, she circles the port over the cooker offering Voicemail connection:

'Direct to Net, site: Violet Life. All Taureans this week.' Seeing Taureans everywhere in the reflective chrome of the ice-cream maker, she begins to let them know some of the things she sees: 'Don't be impatient to have a certain event come to pass. A friend, who may be in a dilemma, may need your guidance and it will be up to you to show this person an error before he or she makes it –'

A distant boom wafts up through the tunnel; a burp of air flips the tunnel-mouth. Vi ignores it. Passing foot-traffic miles away sends out rumbling noises, like giant digestive gurgles, in the intestines leading to town.

'... so don't ignore any of your dreams this week, as each one will deal in a different way with a certain problem you have had for a long time.'

Bubba-bubba-boom. Certainly someone coming this way.

Steady footsteps now, maybe the guy from the 'scope shop again, his arm a little scratched from the blood sample they squeezed out of him the last time he called. Or maybe —

Boom-boom-ker-boom —

'Hi.' Reeve's head appears in the black rubber mouth of the tunnel. Reeve Dunkley has brisk, flat, shining black hair that always goes the way she wants it. 'What are you doing? Horrors again?'

'All Taureans This Week.'

'I'm Cancer. What do I get?'

'The worst-named astrological sign in the calendar?'

'I hate my sign. What do you see?'

Vi sees Reeve being angry. Trusting someone who lets her down. Physical injury is involved, maybe a leg or an ankle. 'All Cancerians This Week. We always think we know a person better than we actually do, where a matter of pride is involved.'

'What's that mean?'

'Watch your leg or your ankle.'

'Anything else?'

'Friends introduce you to someone you can really get to know, perhaps for the rest of your life.'

'That all?'

'For now.'

'What's that — thing on the floor?'

'Protective suit. Heat-welded seams.' Vi resurrects her suit off the kitchen floor. It practically stands up by itself. 'I'm going out in it.'

'Not with me.'

'Outside, out.'

'The Undercliff?'

'The Undercliff, first. Anywhere there's major shade.'

Reeve considers it. 'When?'

'Any day now.'

'Still, Nick —'

'Doesn't have to know. Maps, please,' Vi instructs the nearest port, bringing up a menu on the nearest wall detecting her presence. 'Anderville, 20801 Wills Compound, scale one in four.'

Anderville is the name of the house. In moments it's illuminated by a map of itself on the wall. Surrounding it are worms of black that link it to other compounds and knot where several meet.

'What's that?'

'A map of the rat-runs to town.' Vi scans the wall. 'The nearest place to the Undercliff would be —'

'Bruce's house — here.' Reeve indicates the place.

'Correct.'

'Risky. It's on the Vale.'

Bruce Stallingham lives on Brankshire, where The Vale, which is a listening station, gives out on to a track to the Undercliff. And the Undercliff gives out on to a real, an outdoor, life — a real but shady place, if only dimly remembered.

'Risky or not, I'm not staying in this year.'

Reeve shrugs. 'What makes this year different?'

'Can you remember a summer we didn't stay in?'

'No, but –'

'Think about it,' Vi says. 'The beach? When you were little?'

Reeve dimly remembers the feeling of sand on chafed and sunburned legs. The lush, warm wash of the sea on the beach, where sun-block and hats and Protective Weave vests gradually spoiled the careless hours. Where the din of Advice for Bathers finally hardened to 'Beaches Closed' signs all August; and finally from March to October, as media doctors warned of a temporary hazard to children, that best practice was to stay in. The Big Stay-In began when Violet was four. Now that the Solar Advisory Service closed down early March as well, free access to hills and fields and beaches is something that lives in her mind in a place called *Afterminster*, where no one has to stay in any more, where the sun is warming but normal, and soup steams in mugs before the fire when it finally dims in winter …

'I don't remember,' Reeve says. 'There's *EverGreen* now, and *Lambkin*.'

'Game-replacements for reality?'

'Pretty convincing replacements.'

'Don't you want to go out?'

'I do go out.'

'At night. Or buried in tunnels.'

'Only for nine months each year.'

'Three months of freedom? That's enough?'

'Remember what day it is?' Reeve says finally.

'Tuesday.'

'Wednesday. Self-defence.'

UltraViolet wipes ice-cream from around her mouth in that move of Nick's. 'I forgot. When?'

Reeve gives her the pitying head-shake.

'Actually, now, if you're free?'

Chapter 3
The Howling ————————

'Ready?' Reeve asks.

'Almost.' *Put yourself in my place. Would you give up the woods and the breeze, the freedom to walk to a friend's house, without a fight?* Vi blinks into the mirror; squeezes out an air-bubble with her eyelid and fights to keep the contact lens in place. *Fighting's what I do best. So we can walk to the gym now. But in the howling tunnels, anything can happen ...*

'We're late,' Reeve complains. 'You spent enough time choosing contacts.'

'What are you, the mirror police?'

The girl with the violet eyes pulls on jeans and a sweater. A recent printout of the sun from pictures sent to the Net by a space-telescope looks down from her noticeboard. Those sunspots look like a mouth and two eyes. Nick keeps an eye on those sunspots at www.solarstatus.sunwatch.co.uk. Looks like an orange with cloves in it. A disapproving orange, with spots around its chin.

Recently, sunspots got worse. So did magnetic storms, a result of solar activity. So did alterations in the ozone layer that absorb harmful ultraviolet radiation, a result of magnetic storms.

And the earth's defences are down, right now. Earlier each year the long banks of chlorine-making clouds build over the skyline, ready to destroy more ozone and let in more ultraviolet. Visible in January this year, they're probably at work right now over the shining black network of tunnels that makes up the centre of Condorcet.

'Come on,' Reeve says. 'Let's go.' And she leads the way through the kiss of the kitchen tunnel-flap into another world beyond it.

Inside the black spider, the tunnels whisper and clash. Soon Reeve and UltraViolet leave domestic tunnels behind them and gain the solid *boom* underfoot of the echoing Boulevards. The light slides over their bodies from widely spaced low-energy bulkheads; radon meters gleam luminously between them, monitoring dangerous gases, greening Reeve's face as she stops.

'*Sol! Big Sol!*'

'Oh no!' Reeve groans. 'Tell me I'm hearing things.'

A cry over the heart-thump of the air-conditioning – '*Where's that smile? Sol for you, girl? Big Sol!*'

'Smiley. Can't we go another way?'

'*Sol makes your day. Be cool! Mind how you go!*'

'Which way? Sepulveda?'

'Sepulveda Drive goes way out to Brucie's.'

'We could loop back.'

Louder, now: 'Sol! Big Sol! Lovely smile! And you!'

'Sounds like he's in the Concourse.' Reeve names the filthy intersection marking the centre of town. 'We've got to cross it, somehow.'

'Problem.' Vi sums up: 'Avoid the tunnel vendor blocking our way to a self-defence class we're late for already. Answer?'

'Buy a Sol.'

'We did that already. He keeps you talking for ages.'

'We could just run right past him.'

'Contact with people is such a drag, right?' Vi says a little archly. Smiley's one of few people who actually want to *chat*.

'Who buys papers anyway?'

'Maybe people like them. Specially with solar flares.'

Solar flares aren't trousers, though they might make a nice line, Vi thinks. They're actually gouts of super-charged particles ejected by the sun. Sometimes the gouts of particles upset the earth's electromagnetic field. Sometimes the Net goes down. But *Big Sol* always appears, low-tech ink on paper, still spreading the word on secret food mountains, lost tunnel children, projected ozone depletion – all the dirt on BluScreen Worldwide, and its monopoly of UV-Selective polymers. Nick snorted over the last issue, then used it as toilet paper, also in pretty short supply, like books, tanning oils, cars, non-essential hair products and animals in fields.

'Sol! *Big Sol!* How are you, man? Long time no see.' Smiley corners a man in a hurry. Girls, he watches out for.

Vi strips the rad band off her wrist and extends it outside through a tunnel-vent.

'What are you doing?' Reeve looks up.

'Putting it out in the sun.'

'But you'll rack up –'

'Rads, so what?'

'So you can't go outside if you O.D.'

'Because I can go outside now?' With only twenty hours' full sunlight allowed to register in any one year, UltraViolet has used up plenty already. 'I don't care about radiation records any more. I'm getting out of here this summer, somehow or other.'

'How does this help us pass Smiley?'

Vi winks. 'Wait and see.'

The rad band bakes on the top of the tunnel, turning slowly through orange to red, the span of Violet Niles's wrist bone looking pathetically small. Beneath it the Concourse booms, the spaghetti junction of the central tunnels crossing blasted scrubland as far as a ravine. In the ravine a river blurts through hot rocks two miles to the gloom of the Undercliff, the only shade for miles.

The little town of Condorcet shimmers in the desert, the occasional pool flashing turquoise in the glare of the sun, Blu-domed farms and rat-runs hunkered down under the heat-haze.

White fingers bloom on the top of the black plastic tunnel; scurry across it like a crab.

'Ow! That's hot!' Vi recovers her rad band, a bloody shade of red.

'Thirty rads or over,' Reeve boggles. 'You totally cooked it – why?'

'Girls! Grab a *Sol*, make my day.' Smiley lights up like the sun the moment he spots them. 'When was the last time you gave me that beautiful smile –'

'Thursday?' Reeve says coldly.

'– when you got so much to smile about, looking so fine?'

'Brisk trainers,' Vi notices. Dressed in Blu-Tex sportswear, expensive *Nebula* trainers on his feet, he doesn't look like he relies on the *Sol* to eat. 'How d'you afford them on sales of Big *Sol*?'

Smiley looks at her coolly. 'I got no home to go to, how about you?'

'Yes.' Vi drops her eyes. 'I'm sorry, I didn't mean –'

'No problem. *Sol* for you, girls?'

Some tunnel vendors are a lot more disturbing than Smiley's relentless cheerfulness, hiding problems Vi can only guess at. The sad loner by Wesley Co-op mutely extends the magazine from the depths of an anorak. This guy is hard to forget. But Smiley's fine whether you buy or you don't. It's this that makes him so hard to pass by. So hard to escape from as well.

'We've got one already.'

'Spread the word, keep your mind informed. That big sol in the sky, he's going to be stirring it up, know what I'm saying?'

He advances, pressing a magazine on them.

Vi flashes her rad band. 'I'm Hot, better stay away.'

Smiley backs off instantly, registering the colour of the band in the same glance that tells him that the security cameras above them have registered it too. 'Hey, now. I could lose my licence.'

'Some rebel.' Vi flashes him a smile as she passes without breaking step. 'Can't sell to the Heat, oh no,' she mutters under her breath. 'Wouldn't want to lose our tunnel vendors' licence, even though we *are* selling the *Sol*.'

Smiley smiles uncertainly after them. 'Look after yourself. Be cool.'

'Good one,' Reeve gloats, as they hurry away.

'Did you see, he's *afraid* of me?'

'Afraid of getting Monitored.'

'So?'

'Still, your rads –'

'Don't care any more.'

'They'll section you.'

'How?'

'Confining Order.'

'Like to see them try.'

Reeve bobs along beside Vi, several inches taller than her, sympathetically close. Smiley watches the two figures dwindle away down the Boulevard. That girl, she should mind her sun-manners. A red band for twenty hours plus, and *not even mid-summer yet?*

'We'll be looking at strangles today,' Ken Wen informs the class. 'And what we can do to prevent them.'

Not more than two hundred metres from Smiley's station in the Boulevard, the self-defence class waits to be instructed in the Hothouse Gym, well-named because of its poor ventilation.

'Duck, turn, throw. Ben, can we give it a try?'

Reeve and Vi exchange glances. It's hard not to laugh as poor Ben, who always gets chosen, reluctantly mounts an attack.

Deftly, Wen ducks as Ben tries to strangle him from behind, using Ben's own momentum to throw him to the floor. Ben rises with an effort, charges Wen, locates his hands around Wen's neck. Wen chops Ben's arms off his neck and whips Ben's arm up his back. 'This will immobilize your attacker –' He leans a little on the arm, Ben squeals and claps Wen's back – 'and this will break the joint.'

Wen releases Ben. 'Violet – have we got it?'

'I think we have,' Vi says quickly.

'You are using the power of your attacker against himself. Now – practise. Practise, please.'

Reeve and Vi practise three different escapes from strangles on the mat, over and over again, one eye on the clock and the other on Wen, building up a terrific head of heat, until hands and hair smell of rubber matting, and bodies feel battered and bruised.

At last it's time for focussing.

Wen waits for their attention. He does a lot with his *Ki*, or inner power. His eyes are black and commanding. When he raises his hand, no one speaks.

'Next week, knife attacks. When we are cornered, and there is nothing left to do, we must defend ourselves the best way we can.' His eyes alight on her. 'What do you say, Violet Niles?'

'Never give up, I agree.'

'"Never give up" isn't my meaning.'

'It's my meaning,' UltraVi says.

Ken Wen senses the Ki behind her smile. Violet meets his gaze boldly.

'Our focus this week is Never Give Up.' Wen's eyes rove around the class. One by one, his students look down under his penetrating glance. He bows. 'Until next time.'

'Roll on knife attacks,' Vi mutters, rolling away the mats.

The boy named Ben looks at her. 'See you,' he says a bit glumly, flexing his aching arm. Violet watches him go. She would have fought back, herself.

On leaving the Hothouse Gym the air has a different quality. The tunnels are warm on re-entry into the rat-runs, plus there's a sound on the air, filling the sonorous distances, louder on the turn to the Boulevard.

Aroo — roo —

'What's that?'

Vi listens. 'A baby crying?'

'Some animal in pain?'

They listen again.

'Who knows?'

They make a right on to the Anderville tunnel, and the howling seems to pursue them; the cry of something sick and mournful, magnified and thrown back by the booming echoes in the tunnels, it's the sound of the last thing on earth howling under the moon.

'Why won't it go away?'

'Coming closer.'

'It's following us,' Reeve panics.

Vi licks her lips. 'It's between us and my house.'

Ow — ow — arroooooah-arroo! Arooah! Arooah! AROOO —

'What are we going to do?' Reeve claps her hands over her ears.

'Go round by Sepulveda?'

'Brucie's place?'

AROOAH–AROOAH–AROO—

'Quick, it's coming closer!' Reeve starts to run as she says it. 'Quick!' Reeve screams. 'Vi, *run!*'

Chapter 4

The Vale————————

'What's up, Brucie – a bomb hit the place?'

Bruce Stallingham surveys the wreckage of the family kitchen in a slightly more bewildered way than usual. 'Want a shake?' he offers. 'I can make one.'

'What else have you got?' Reeve shudders, not only at the memory of the howling, left behind at last in the tunnel out to Sepulveda Drive, but at the sight of the kitchen worksurfaces.

Bruce looks at them helplessly. 'I was just about to clear up.'

'Got any Power Mix?'

'Fruit and nuts?' Brucie looks dubious. 'Carrots.'

'If that's all you've got.'

'Carrots,' Bruce says again.

'Can we secure this tunnel?' Vi says.

'Where did you say it came from?' Stallingham ignores her. 'That howling, I mean?'

'Somewhere round our house. I told you.'

'It followed us,' Reeve adds. 'It almost followed us here.'

'Did it sound like a person?'

Reeve shudders again. 'No way was this thing human.'

The rubber flap over the tunnel mouth bulges and relaxes with changing movements and pressures transmitted through the tunnel network, some of them many hundreds of metres distant. None of this seems to reach Brucie. Vi rescues a broken bowl from the floor. 'Here — someone might step on it.'

Bruce examines it. 'You startled me.'

'You didn't hear us coming?'

Evidently not, since he dropped his bowl of cereal the second before they came in. Vi takes in the exploded Wheeties and fragments of china over the floor, the dog-biscuits over the mat, the sink full of dishes and tea-towels, the exhausted stove choked with ashes; Bruce's face, unwashed, grim plugs of gunk in his eyes. Remembering something, he rummages in a sack. 'Carrot?'

'No thanks, I don't.'

'Looks like someone strangled you.'

'Self-defence at the Hothouse.' Vi rubs the bruise on her neck.

Bruce takes a bite of his carrot. 'They ought to be more careful.'

'Who?'

'Whoever strangled you.'

'It was me,' says Reeve. The freaky noises in the tunnels make the idea of self-defence class the best thing they did in a long time. She meets Vi's eyes. *Arooo-arragh—*

Vi puts her ear to the tunnel-flap. 'Will this exit secure any better?'

Brucie swallows. 'Unhitch, you mean?'

'If you have to.'

'I don't, before Solstice Day.'

'But could you?' Vi persists.

'Suppose. When Dad gets back.'

'Where is he?'

'Wesley Co-op.'

'Rice or flour?'

'Potatoes.'

'Overnight then.'

'Maybe.'

Wesley Co-op, that thundering, empty-aisled food station, crashing with the arrival of crates that appear and disappear, where time seems to stand still and queues form for toilet paper. Vi groans inwardly. Potato queues are always spectacular. Best to go armed with a sleeping bag. You can expect to bed down in the Minster Mall for a first shot at rice or potatoes, that's if they're actually there when you reach the head of the queue. Wesley can swallow you whole for a day and spit you out with something you didn't really want, for the price of something you did. A sack of navy beans; cracked, grey pasta; cans of tuna with 'dolphin friendly' symbols; ancient, gummy marmalade; dusty lentils, oddities like canned custard, bright orange and well over dates.

'Why would I unhitch, anyway?' Bruce wonders mildly.

The howling. 'Scarey out there,' Vi says. 'Hard to explain, but —'

'There's vagrants,' Reeve says.

'What's vagrants?'

'People with no fixed abode.'

'Like Stevie.' Stallingham names his younger brother.

'People – things – could come in.'

'Let them,' Bruce says blankly.

Vi applies lip-balm. 'You all right, Bruce?'

Bruce examines the ceiling. 'Are you?'

On the ceiling above Bruce, a fly senses the knife covered in apricot jam in the sink beside Reeve's left elbow. Above the fly and the ceiling, loft insulation cooks in the roof overhead, as the sun beats down on the gables. Above the sizzling roof-tiles, the remains of Virginia Creeper, still clinging to the chimney, crisp and curl in the sun. Above the chimney a clear blue sky hums with reflected heat.

There was a time on Sepulveda Drive, the rock daisies bloomed like gems; powder-pink, baby-blue and every shade of mauve, twenty years ago they clung in colourful mats over every fold and crevice along the ocean boulevard. Now the daisy, or day's eye, has had to close itself against too much light from the sun. Daisyless rocks tumble down to the sea and the cracked and empty highway rolls on, car-less as well, on its long meander to the city from its beginnings deep in the Vale.

Brucie's place, at the head of the Vale, overlooks the fluffy green worm of the Undercliff, shaded beneath limestone overhangs. Beyond it a single fluffy island sits in the flashing blue sea, a landslip that calved off the Undercliff, one stormy night, many years ago. Now gulls roost on

Hume Island, deep in the sheltering shade. Seabirds nesting in the open have long since disappeared.

The skies above Brucie's place aren't empty, nevertheless. Hard to miss the pristine white dishes, catching international messages. Brankshire Vale scans e-mail for national security purposes. Buzzwords triggering surveillance include the words *Big Sol* and *Random Squires*.

Bruce rolls his eyes. 'They're listening, you know.'

'They are?'

'The Vale. They'll find Stevie better than I can.'

Stevie again. 'He went somewhere?'

'Missing since yesterday.'

'Where did he go?'

'If I knew that, I could have found him.' Brucie goes slightly pink.

Reeve shrugs. 'He won't go far.'

'He made a break for the Undercliff,' Vi says.

'How do you know?'

'Where else is there to go?'

'He probably racked up a million rads,' Bruce says miserably.

'Mum?'

'Visiting friends.'

'Emergency services?'

'Confining Order, if we alert them.'

'See what you mean.' Vi thinks. 'Then we get him tonight, before they do.'

'You mean – go outside?'

Vi smiles the Smiley smile. 'What have we got to lose?'

'Leave the tunnel,' Reeve says. 'Stevie might come back.'

'He won't use the tunnel.'

'How do you know?'

'Cameras at major junctions,' Vi says. 'Would you come in that way?'

The tunnel-flap bulges again and a faint echo of anxiety stirs in Bruce's mind. Where the tunnel never meant much before except the summer exit to town, now its unzippable smile seems like a fatal flaw in the family fortress. Rolling out a metal tunnel-cap from behind the kitchen door, Brucie secures it with flanges that snap around the tunnel-mouth like teeth.

'Suppose your dad comes back?' Reeve objects.

'He can call me. Let's Quest.'

'How much time do we have?'

Vi slips off the table. 'Dark at eight-thirty. That gives us three hours.'

'So where are you?' Bruce becomes almost chatty as he leads them upstairs to his room.

'Where are you?'

'Usher Wood.'

'Three dials?'

'The Holm Oak.'

'Jamie Steele got further,' Reeve says.

'I know someone who got out of the wood altogether.'

'So what's beyond it? The Speckled Band?'

'How do I know? I told you, I haven't got there yet.'

They Quest in separate levels, separate worlds. Isolation's the problem, even in cyber space. It's a national phenomenon. Help-lines won't help you. Families can't help each other. Electronic education won't help you, as you find out more and more, and experience less and less, of the shrinking world outside.

Nothing can replace a day at the beach together, sandy and carefree, that day the sea lies waiting for you below the cliff-path, that delicious sense of excitement as you race full-tilt down the zigzag, your flip-flops flipping as you go. Only the rain in your face can convince you the weather forgave you, that the sun's going to let you come out like some flower, so that beaches can fill and neighbours chat over fences, the way they used to do. 'Ludostipation' is just the latest silly buzzword for a condition known as living indoors, an obsession with electronic games, an inability to connect ...

Meanwhile *QuestHolme* provides the next best thing to excitement. Trail X, through Usher Wood and beyond, throws lights in the players' faces, each wall throwing up a 'courtesy' screen, blocking sight of the others.

Exclamations and curses ring out. The girl with the violet eyes and her excitable friends could be madmen, if they weren't locked in different worlds, responding to multiple action.

'Oh. You wish.'

'Die, you — Yes! No! Yes!'

'Shoot! Dream on! No, you don't!'

The hour for setting out on the quest for Stevie comes and goes. Six and a half hours have passed, when by midnight it has to be *Cohorts* which is the game of choice.

A reconstruction of the battle of Carthage, it winks up on the kitchen wall, continuous with the bedroom wall overhead. Behind the broken crockery and overflowing sink, pillars topple against a Mediterranean sky as the Romans raze Carthage and plough salt into the ground. Unless, of course, you can stop them.

Behind the frantic soundtrack, a scraping sound can be heard.

The metal cap sealing the tunnel-mouth moves very slightly. A whining sound. More scraping, claws on metal. Finally the sound of howling, diminishing into the distance.

Brucie shudders upstairs over the clash of steel against shield. Perhaps from the depths of Carthage and beyond, the faintest echo of disquiet reaches him as, between zapping Romans, he begins to eat the carrot he finds, for some reason, in his hand.

Not very far from Brucie's place, a motorcycle waits under the moon.

'Some of the things they come up with,' a lone figure tells its helmet radio. 'One guy makes a break over the valley, ground like a skillet, two miles from any shade. I pull the guy over, he looks at me, like, What? I'm guessing he has a good reason for grilling his hide, like his wife's in labour or something.'

Solar Adviser Bo Headingley dismounts, kicks out the stand on the bike, walks and talks to her radio, shaking her head, her boots crunching lizard skeletons to powder on the cold, dry valley floor.

'Turns out he's out in full sol to fetch his partner's golf clubs from some godforsaken trailer park! That has to be the worst reason I ever heard. You got thirty rads, I tell him. You better stay indoors.'

It's the third night of a three-night shift. Moonlight glancing off her helmet, Bo Headingley patrols Condorcet limits, having slept badly during the day in her airless trailer. A headache beats under her helmet. Any Leakers tonight can be sure of a sharp reception. No way will she suffer fools gladly.

'Then two weeks later, he tries it again. What can you do but Advise 'em?'

And fools they are, those who travel by night. They don't think Best Practice is to stick to your area food co-op? This area's co-op is Wesley. With transport limited, there have to be rules. And the Solar Advisory Service is there to Advise that Best Practice is to follow them.

'You won't believe what they tell you. I left my wallet on the grass. I'm waiting for someone. I fell asleep. I thought ten minutes wouldn't harm me. I'm wearing sunblock, see? Joe Public wants to do *what he wants to do*. Same with smoking and speeding, now it's sunbathing − how come everything bad for you has to begin with an S?' She laughs. 'Sausages, for sure. You wish. Over and out.'

Headingley scans the horizon on a moonlit night, with the ocean stretching dimly beyond the Vale. Night patrols, you don't get much movement here, usually. The Vale's enough to deter all but the boldest Leaker. Under the listening dishes, nothing stirs but a mouse. On second thoughts, make that a cricket. Dormice went extinct a while ago. Crickets exist. Of course they do. Yeah, and they come indoors.

A lot of things come indoors, now the world got simmered in a pan. Slugs and snails, bats and beetles, crane-flies, swifts, even jack-rabbits. Headingley sighs. The thought of her bunk in the trailer is pretty appealing right now. Spiders are fine in their place, but dropping on to your face during the day, when you're catching some zeds after a night shift? Animals outside, people in. That's the way it should be.

Home is usually a clearing under the trees at Thoreau Place, a crumbling old mansion guarding the only pond for miles around. Tonight Headingley's trailer sits on Sepulveda Drive. Sikesie probably trashed it by now, if he isn't asleep.

Sikes, he likes to sleep. Also he likes to eat just about anything he can get his teeth into, including a poisonous plant on the Undercliff one time, which very nearly sent him to Big Dog Camp in the sky. Leave him at home for a change, you can guarantee there'll be –

Headingley narrows her eyes. A form flickers over the desert.

You won't believe what they tell you ...

Headingley brings her hands to her mouth. 'Hey, you! Joe Leaker! Stop!' Out of the corner of her eye she spots another fleeing figure; three figures altogether, flickering between the open, moonlit scrub and the shadows thrown by the rocks. 'That'll do it! Stop now!' The figures duck and weave, faster now they heard her, making a desperate break for cover in the direction of the dense black outline of the Undercliff.

'You're not going to make it!' But they are, without Sikes to run them down. 'I Advise you to STOP RIGHT NOW!'

Nothing but a swaying salt-bush indicates their path.

'Seems like they came from Sepulveda, could be the Stallingham compound,' Headingley tells her radio. 'Three Leakers, the Vale, one-fifty-three a.m., possibly two male, one female ...'

No need to attempt to follow them, Headingley knows from experience. Be back before you can say 'broiler chickens' with horribly sunburned faces, sorry and sore, not too much to say for themselves. We felt like picking flowers. We went for a walk in the moonlight, thought we could get back before the sun came up. I'm sorry, you mean we're Confined?

Headingley shakes her head. Only been an Adviser nine months, heard every excuse under the sun. Leakers by night, that's a Caution. Leakers by day, that's a Confining Order, depending on the number of rads. She picked up a few rads herself from Advising during the day. Night duty, that's easier – except for the temperature. Headingley lights a small fire and warms her hands. A Leaker's fire is an offence on this tinder-dry valley floor. An Adviser's fire, that's different. And with no clouds in the sky, when the sun goes down the desert loses heat as fast as a man without a hat.

Something rushes by her.

'Best Practice is listen to Advice!' Headingley drops her hands. What *was* that? 'Hey, I'm talking to you – come back!'

Arrooah — alloooo — rooo —

Some kind of howling, somewhere?

Looo — looo — aroooooh …

These wild dogs, they know how to spook you. Headingley shudders. Turns up her collar. The stars overhead look bright and unkind as the poor earth rolls over, toasting its other side in the sun, grilling tender continents each and every day.

After a while she stamps out her fire.

These Leakers, they think they can get away with it. Specialists in solar exposure have studied its effects for years. Advice is there to help them, and they think they can come and go as they want? One out, all out, then where will Solar Drill be? 'A Thousand Crisped in Condorcet', she guesses *Big Sol* will read.

But that isn't going to happen. Those Leakers are in for a surprise. Wait till they find their return path blocked by a very large rottie indeed. Sikes can be very persuasive. They'll be ill-Advised not to consider a little lecture on sun manners …

Headingley fires up the bike. Reaching the trailer on weed-filled Sepulveda Drive, once the Scenic Ocean Boulevard teeming with surfies and tourists, she throws down the bike and flings wide the door. It's then that the smell hits her.

'Sikes! You drank my beer!'

The Rottie shakes his head, the home-brew Headingley

had left in a tub flying from his chops like foam. Headingley rescues a pill-container. Something grits under her feet. Blood-coloured pills all over the floor, quite a few of them missing. 'My Vit. D – what have you *done?*'

Sikes thumps his tail and sneezes, pleased he made an effort.

'Bo to Advisory Centre.' Headingley keeps her voice steady, as videophone gives her Harriet. 'Harry, my dog just ate fifty micrograms, times thirty, of Vitamin D – what would be the effect on a medium-to-large Rottweiler?'

'No effect,' yawns Harriet at mission control.

'You know that?'

'Body excretes the excess.'

'Thought too much D was dangerous.'

'Not in dogs.'

'You sure?'

'Do you have a report or what?'

'Three Leakers out at the Vale, travelling Undercliff direction.' Sikes rolls on the bunk. Headingley slaps him affectionately. He looks a little foamy around the mouth, but what's new? 'Moving to cover the area by day, with a view to apprehend and Advise. Night, Harry. I'm grabbing five.'

'Best Practice is to go now. No opportunity to promote good sun manners can responsibly be ignored.'

'Textbook stuff.'

'You should know, you just did all the tests.'

'OK, I'm on my way.'

Headingley hitches the bike to the back of the trailer; flips the catches on a BluScreen awning that snaps on to the roof. Holding her nose against the yeasty smell of unready beer, she enters the driving seat and pats the place beside her.

'Sikesie – front seat. Good dog.'

For some reason a strange song occurs to her as she engages first gear on a highway she can guarantee to have all to herself: 'The deep blue sea, the deep blue sea, there's a lot to see in the deep blue sea. The glass-bottom boat, you will agree, can show you the wonders of the deep blue sea ...'

Where in the world did *that* come from?

'The flying fish is an awful ham, three-point landing in a frying pan ... the deep blue sea, the deep blue sea, there's a lot to see in the deep blue sea ...'

Singing under a fiery dawn over the ocean boulevard, the dog Sikes beside her crazed on home brew, Bo Headingley, Solar Adviser, heads the trailer back to the Vale.

Some people don't know what's good for them.

No other way out from the Undercliff except a dive off the cliffs into the sea. All other routes lie under the listening dishes. Those leakers'll have to re-cross the desert sometime to the cluster of blisters known as Condorcet.

And when they do, she and Sikes, well –

they'll be ready for 'em.

Chapter 5

The Break————————

'Run! Break towards the bushes!'

'I can't!'

'You can do it – come on – run!'

UltraVi runs on herself, leaving Reeve to follow her as best she can. Run, dip, dive to the cover of a rock throwing a long shadow behind it across the moonlit desert floor.

Wait here a little. Brucie?

Vi turns to spot Reeve scuttling towards her over the scrub, the moon glimmering, almost full, overhead. Risky under the dishes. But Stevie came by the Vale. In the full light of day, no less. No way can they leave Bruce to face this alone. Together they'd stormed Carthage most of the night. Now they need to help him find Stevie, also alone and probably shell-shocked, in the wilds of the Undercliff.

It isn't the first time Violet Niles has leaked from a compound by night. But never so far and so freaky. The others had taken persuading, Bruce especially. But once the moon had glimmered outside with a promised spell of freedom, and the bite of the night air wafted smells and tastes forgotten for ever on the tick of a breeze thick with insects, the taste of adventure reached even Brucie. Can't get sunburned at night, right? Right, Bruce. Not under the moon. Reeve had welcomed the night air. Be back before morning, right? With luck, certainly we will. Reeve had grinned. So come on, then. What are we waiting for?

Now the adventure's real, the open ground lit by the moonlight looks bare as a ... UltraVi searches her mind for a wide open space, and finds none from being inside all her life. Well, as bare as a head with no hair on it.

With a spray of dust, Reeve skids into place beside her.

'Brucie?'

'On his way.'

Behind Reeve, Condorcet winks on the desert, its generators working overtime to circulate some air through its shared respiratory systems. Shoppers sleep fitfully in the Minster Mall outside Wesley Co-op, stewing slowly in their sleeping bags. The boys' father, John Stallingham, dreams of potatoes in his sleep, his coat chocked under his head and his NetCredit cards under that. Rice and Flour coupons can be exchanged first thing if he's lucky.

'I don't see him.'

'Yet.'

'Where is he?'

Reeve scans the dense block of blackness ahead, as a smaller block rushes to meet it. 'Ahead of us – there!'

'Hurry, or we'll lose him.'

'I'm calling Nick.'

'Now?'

'I leave it too late, he rings round.' Stabbing QuikDial on

her watch display, Vi makes a dash for the nearest rock. Hunkers down. 'Dad?'

'Hey.'

The moon glimmers over the desert floor. Next bit looks tricky – no cover.

'I'm at Reeve's.'

'Self-defence today?'

'This morning.'

'Right.'

A small rock. Good. Now for the open ground.

'Thought you might wonder where I was.'

'You sound a little breathless – everything OK?'

Reeve ducks down beside her. Vi pushes her on – 'Go!'

'What are you doing?'

'Playing QuestHolme.'

'You sure?'

Reeve dodges under the moon. A shout rings out – STOP RIGHT NOW! – but Reeve dodges on, ducking, diving, disappearing, her figure melting at last into the darkness under the trees.

'I'm staying over. I have to go.'

Time for her own break now. Vi begins the run across open ground.

'Vi?'

'What?'

'You running?'

'No, I just made a bad move.'

'Questing, you mean? What level?'

Run! Again! Faster! Something overtakes her, a shadow or

a wolf, something black with teeth, who knows, all that matters is *running*! Getting away from the glare of the moon! Vi finally throws herself down. In the blackness Reeve lies waiting.

'Reeve?'

'Here.'

'See that thing?'

'Big wild dog or something?'

'What wild dog?' Vi's wrist demands sharply.

'The Guardian from Edition Six,' UltraViolet improvises wildly, heart pounding against the sand. 'Get past Cerberus to reach the Caverns of the Moon.'

'Reeve there?'

'Say, "Hi".' Vi puts her wrist to Reeve's mouth.

Reeve clears her throat. 'Nick, you know when you look through a microscope and when you try to focus, everything looks kind of exploded?'

'Electron?'

'Light.'

'Could be the focus-puller.'

'That's what I was afraid of.'

'Sounds kind of serious, but try the puller first.'

Way to handle a parent. Vi tries to shut him down: 'Reeve's mum just brought us cocoa –'

Reeve makes slurping noises.

'The moon's almost full tonight – see it?'

'Yes, Dad. Whatever.'

'Affects your horoscopes, doesn't it?'

'Call you soon, OK?'

Vi kills the call. 'Nice distraction technique.'

Reeve grins. 'I thank you.'

Vi examines the terrain ahead, hidden under the black and mysterious bulk of the first truly wild place that waits for them under its own jagged outline under the stars. 'Through these trees and we're there.'

Reeve swats a mosquito. 'I don't think I can do this.'

'We can do anything.' Vi turns around. 'Look what we did, already.'

Behind them the glimmering desert and the lighted domes of Condorcet make an alien landscape not at all like home.

Reeve shakes her head. 'Never seen it like this before.'

'In winter?'

'Never at night.'

'Funny, isn't it?'

'Small.'

'Stevie's probably back already,' Vi says airily.

'If he isn't, d'you think we can find him?'

'He's probably scared – why not?'

The descent to the wilds of the Undercliff shows them Bruce waiting under the moon. 'Someone shouted Stop!' Bruce says. 'Maybe we should go back.'

'Couldn't have seen us properly,' Vi says. 'Come on, it's totally brisk out here – what are we waiting for?'

Reeve leads the way between deep clefts of limestone, her voice flattening as she goes. 'Mind these rocks – they're loose.' The sea falls in little crashes somewhere beyond and below. A rock dislodged by her foot rattles away down the path. She tests the sound of her voice, turning to throw it behind her: 'Mum probably thinks I revised all evening.'

'Online module paper?'

'Tomorrow — today, in fact.'

'She wouldn't have missed you at dinner?'

'We don't have dinner.'

'She won't check your room?'

'My mother in my room, are you kidding?'

Reeve's parents stay out of her room, with its wall-high Questcharacters. Little do they know, as they sleep under the security console, she's running free under the moon. Instead of game-playing alone in her room like every normal teenager, Reeve breathes the stars, the night. Exquisite smells on the air! The sea, the earth, plants, woods, something in the sky — the smell of dawn? A big wide smell, not a puny room with pencils and pens in order.

'What's funny?' Vi says.

'My exams.'

'Because ...?'

'Doesn't seem important, out here. I'm meant to be home revising like a good student with rads to spare, but right now the system wouldn't recognize me, except as a radiation hazard.' Reeve turns to Vi with glittering eyes. 'The path gets narrower — ready?'

No time to look up. Every step down the rubble-littered gully demands complete attention. All around them breathe plants and mosses. This place will always be sheltered. Here growing things can thrive. UltraViolet 'sees' the undergrowth growing over them, rising and ebbing with the years, a tide of growth that will never stop, thanks to the shade of the Undercliff. *No accident we came here.* The Undercliff is more than a chance landslip, more than some shady place a friend's brother ran away to, more than a night adventure, then home to forget all about it. *We were meant to run under this moon. I came here a couple of winters ago — and in my dreams since then* ...

'What are you thinking?' Reeve says.

'Look at that sky.' Bruce whistles.

All along the horizon shafts of light pierce banks of cloud, rosy and backlit from heaven.

'Dawn,' Vi supposes.

'Cloudy, with luck.'

'Sun'll come up, then we'll see.'

Reeve, UltraViolet and Brucie, on the brink of their first summer dawn! Together they reach the green gloom of the Undercliff beeches, hearing, for the first time they can remember, the rustle of tender leaves in the breeze overhead. Vi looks back just once, probing the darkness behind them still lingering over the desert.

It seems to her there's someone watching. A distant figure, moonlight flashing off its helmet. Watching her, watching them. For a moment they face one another across real, and imagined, landscapes.

Then one of them turns to go.

'What is it?' Reeve says.

'Nothing.' Vi keeps the heart-thump of knowledge to herself. Turns and follows Brucie. Someone saw them.

Someone in a helmet. Helmets aren't good. How quickly can they find Stevie and get home double-quick, to Quest over blackcurrant ice-cream? 'Do blackcurrants grow wild?'

Brucie frowns. 'Dunno.'

'When do blackberries come?'

'Sometime soon,' Bruce thinks. 'Not sure what they look like though.'

'But they grow in places like this, don't they?' Remembering what blackberries look like suddenly seems important. 'Why can't we find some now?'

'Aren't they a bit like raspberries?' Reeve says.

Brucie overtakes her. 'Who cares about blackberries? Come on.'

They probably don't come till autumn, of course. Vi gets it straight in her mind. Getting muddled with cyber spring, where everything comes when you want it. A smell-memory of blackberry jelly, lustrous, purple-black, the concentrated taste of summer, quivering on a hunk of bread, brings Vi a picture of her grandmother gathering blackberries on the common, her hands purple-red with their juice.

'Wait for me!'

Still unable to picture blackberries for some reason, dismayed at her dismal lack of knowledge, UltraViolet plunges, unused and confused, into her deep and natural world.

Chapter 6
Stevie

'What's that?'

'Birdsong.'

Bruce stops to listen. 'That's what it is – birds?'

'I think it might be a lark.' Vi scans the sky. 'There – see it?'

The song burbles down from a speck overhead, an uninterrupted succession of trills and flourishes, dipping and rising, never failing, on a thrilling and joyful theme.

'There's a pattern.' Vi thinks she detects it.

'There is?'

'Three whistles – every now and then.'

On every side of the descending path the undergrowth seems alive with sudden twitters and blurts, liquid trills and whistles.

'Dawn chorus,' Reeve thinks she remembers.

'Didn't know birds were so loud,' Brucie grumbles. 'Why don't they stay in bed?'

A little stream draining the cliff-face rushes along beside them, and at last they enter the gloom of the Undercliff proper.

'Wow, it's like Usher Wood!'

Brucie looks up in wonder at trees that remind him of the only other wood in leaf he can remember, the golden glades of the Quest. Above him the dawning light shows a canopy of green: beeches, dressed in spring splendour, under a precipice of limestone white as bone, flushed rose under the rising sun.

'You mean Usher Wood is like this,' UltraViolet corrects him. 'This is reality, remember?'

'I can't believe we're outside – feels like inside, here.' Reeve leads the way along the dank path, matted into a smooth surface like unbaked clay by the passage of animals' feet – she supposes, by animals' feet. 'Look at these ferns.'

'Freaky.'

Mutant Hart's Tongue ferns, the tip of each leaf ballooning into one or two 'fingers', appear on either side of the path. Vi scans ahead, looking for 'normal' ferns. 'They tried to grow three ways at once, then changed their minds,' she decides.

'Look for tracks!' Brucie slips ahead, flurrying rooks from a cleft over the path, sending them cawing and scolding over the trees. *Raw! Raw! Recaw!*

'It so reminds me of *Ravendale*.' Vi watches them circle overhead. 'Gothic Quest, where ravens attack and you get the jewelled mace?'

'Gets you on to the Castle Gorm, where the mace unlocks a QuestKey.'

'If Seshwan doesn't show. Feels like we're Questing, doesn't it?'

'Spooky,' Reeve agrees.

Bruce rejoins them. 'See any tracks?'

'On this path, are you kidding?'

The densely compacted path resists the mark of their feet, as it must have resisted Stevie's. Though the younger Stallingham might have slipped between them moments before, the strange balloony fingers of the outstretched Hart's Tongue ferns betray no sign of his passing. It might be the church of spring, so hushed is the atmosphere; like the walls of some great cathedral, the limestone buttresses and leafy fretwork above them seem to send the world away and heighten every sensation.

'See that?'

A little further on, and Hume Island appears below them, fields and woods that fell into the sea and became another country, lashed by waves trapped in the gulf between it and the cliff it slipped from.

Reeve stops to watch them foaming. 'Would he come this far?'

'Why not?'

'Stevie'd go anywhere,' Brucie confirms. 'He isn't afraid of anything.'

Vi pictures Stevenson Stallingham, a more daring version of Bruce. Fair, blue-eyed, his smile a little wonky due to uneven teeth, always in nervous motion – he's hard to recall in detail except as a lively blur. 'You don't think ... that howling ...'

'I told you, it isn't human,' Reeve insists.

It isn't anything human that waits for them in the rhubarb

patch. It's some kind of QuestElf or pixie, sitting under a giant rhubarb leaf with a stick and an evil grin, like some twisted flower fairy. The stems are studded with giant purple prickles and hold leaves the size of cafe umbrellas. It takes a moment to register there's a normal-sized boy underneath.

The boy sneers. 'How long did it take you to find me?'

'Steve … you … Stee-vie!'

Bruce bolts and strangles him. They roll and fight in the leaves, losing one another, closing again. Finally Bruce headlocks Stevie, casually picking prickles from his clothing and parking them in Stevie's hair. Stevie struggles free, stands panting and kicking the 'rhubarb' stems.

Vi touches them. 'Get these leaves.'

'That's funny, is it? Waiting here?' Reeve doesn't think much of it.

The elf of giant rhubarb grins. 'Heard you coming a mile off. You're not exactly stealthy.'

Bruce snaps him on the arm. 'Do that again, you can stay here.'

The spikes of the giant rhubarb may or may not carry a mild poison, but they're certainly sharp to the touch, like the needles of oversized brambles or the claws of some giant animal. This spot in the Undercliff is touched with giantism. Enormous ferns sprawl over huge colonies of rock-plants; above hangs the craggy profile of the cliff-face, its hooked nose dwarfing everything else and muddling any sense of scale.

'What's with hiding in this stuff?' Bruce tries to tear a rhubarb leaf.

Stevie shrugs. 'Knew you'd stop here.'

'So why did you go?' Reeve presses.

A sea-breeze stirs the rhubarb and the leathery leaves clack together. Suddenly Stevie darts off. Brucie crashes after him. 'Oh, no, I don't think so.'

When Vi and Reeve catch up with them, there's a stand-off on the edge of the cliff, on a nose of land named The Beak. Stevie teases on the edge. Brucie chucks stones into the sea. 'Anytime you're ready. We only have to get back before Dad calls the police.'

The swell crashes on Hume Island below. Tracks are visible among its rocks, where the descendants of marooned goats still come and go. Crops were tilled there and harvested from the crazily tilted fields, even after it fell into the sea, by people reluctant to lose land to the ocean. But the sea won in the end. Gradually no one bothered to cultivate the island's forty-five-degree slopes any more, and at last the goats took over. Now the goats are scabby and cankerous and no one counts them or tends them, or cares how many are left.

'Mouldy old goats.' Stevie kicks a stone off The Beak. It rattles away down the cliff-face and disappears into the sea. 'Someone should go over there and shoot them.'

'Come back,' Reeve urges. 'You're in the sun.'

'Told you, I'm not coming back.'

Brucie strips a grass stem casually. 'So what, you're going to live here?'

Could someone live here? How? Vi looks at the sun, fully

risen now over the sea; the heat shimmering over the waves in irridescent colours, ultraviolet radiation almost visibly penetrating its surface, killing plankton to a depth of a metre.

'I'm coming back for carrots,' Stevie says at last.

'For food, and everything else.'

'I like it outside. What's wrong with it here?'

'You can't live here, is what's wrong.'

'You could – with a garden,' Vi says.

Stevie comes out of the sun a little. 'Yes, with a garden.'

'No, with a garden.' Reeve looks at them pityingly.

Bruce checks his watch. 'We should get back.'

'Come on,' Reeve says. 'Let's go.'

'Not in full sol.'

'Yes, in full sol – my on-line exam, remember?'

'I forgot, I brought some Approveds.' Bruce shakes sunglasses out of his jacket.

'You thought ahead.'

'From last year.' He hands Vi a pair. 'Sorry if they're scratched.'

Reeve dons them reluctantly. 'They could do nice-looking Approveds.'

'And make them better-fitting, why would they want to do that?' Vi slips on her shades. White faces, dark glasses, looking at one another. Ahead, a daring run under the sun. 'Ready?'

'Those rads,' Brucie worries.

'We could go back when its dark,' Vi suggests. 'Why not stay for the day?'

'Missed my last exam,' Reeve says. 'I'm not missing out on this one.'

'That's worth getting sunburned for.'

'Can't cross under full sol,' Bruce says. 'Even with shades. Not really.'

'Use what you have around you, right?' Stevie looks cool and glamorous with a pair of Approveds hiding his eyes. He could be almost anyone, almost any age. 'You should know that from the Quest.'

'You're telling us what to do now?' Vi puts her hands on her hips.

'Ignore him,' Bruce says.

'It's you we came to rescue in the first place.'

'Don't need rescuing.'

'Do.'

'Rescue yourself,' Stevie says.

'Call your dad.' UltraVi pushes her wristphone at Stevie. 'Tell him you ran away, how we're stuck on the Undercliff.'

'Tell him yourself.' Stevie darts away up the path.

'Steve, she didn't mean it! Steve! Wait! Come back!'

Bruce leads the chase through the Undercliff, through marshy places and stinging things; across streams; behind boulders; over ledges and fallen trees; across slippery stepping stones and under overhangs until, panting, they throw themselves down.

'I hate you, you know that?' Bruce sits on Stevie.

'How good does that make me feel?' Stevie and Bruce punch one another weakly, gradually subsiding as the mood of the place descends; above them the beech tops wagging in the breeze, around them the mossy breath of growing things.

'I'm bringing my frogs here,' Vi decides.

'Frogs?' someone asks, at last.

'My frogs I raise in the bath.'

A pause.

'Why the bath?'

'It's cool. I keep their tank there.'

Coolness. Tanks. The bath. Their thoughts spin away in the timeless gloom of the Undercliff, where dreams grow like mushrooms in the dark while real things fly by and scream. Like the quarters marking a clock face, they lie and look up at the sky, Reeve at twelve o'clock, Bruce at a quarter-past, Stevie at half-past the hour, Vi at a quarter-to.

How good does this make me feel? The shifting lacework of leaves above her fills UltraVi with delight. How completely and utterly good it feels to lie here, happy, scratched and exhausted, after a chase through woods and rocks; how completely right to lie and look up at the cloudless blue sky and let your thoughts drift away...

'We have to get back,' Reeve says dreamily.

'Where are we?' Vi lifts her head.

'Top of the path,' Bruce reckons. 'Not far from home, in fact.'

'Sun's overhead,' Vi murmurs. 'Hottest part of the day.'

Stevie appears with a rhubarb leaf. 'Use what's around you, right?'

Vi sits up. 'Where did you get that?'

He holds it over him like a giant umbrella. 'Rhubarb.'

'Same to you.'

'You need a leaf to wrap around the stem, but the spikes still hurt a bit.' Stevie shifts his grasp on the prickly stem. He jumps on a rock, waves the leaf up and down like a slave boy fanning a maharajah under some eastern sky, instead of the boss of them all. '*Told* you I always know what to do, you should all follow me!'

Chapter 7

Fully Advised————

Bo Headingley adjusts her binoculars and tries to believe her eyes.

What's that prophesy in *Macbeth*, when it looks like a wood moves, or something, then Macbeth goes crazy? *When Birnam Wood comes to Dunsinane...*

Headingley rubs her eyes and reapplies the bins. No doubt about it now. Over the plain swimming with heat, comes a ... moving patch of *rhubarb*.

She thinks about calling control, saying, 'Rhubarb advancing.'

Sikesie strains on his leash, rumbling with hate and distrust of whatever it is coming towards them like a moving oasis of green.

'Something weird, three o'clock to the trailer, just about midday ...' Keeping her eye on the mirage ahead, Headingley talks to her radio. 'Big ... green ... kind of saucer-shaped. Can't tell what it is yet. Investigating anyway, with a view to identify and Advise.'

The last recorded report from Solar Adviser Bo

Headingley, this message will be replayed many times and no one will know what it means.

'That's some major rhubarb.' Headingley pinches herself. Four giant leaves with legs. The legs begin to look less threatening, the nearer they approach.

'You got no chance! Come on!' Headingley hails them through a megaphone.

She guesses the legs didn't see her; for a moment they look as though they'll run.

'Over here! Take it slow!'

The rhubarb approaches slowly.

'OK, let me see those faces!'

The giant leaves rise slowly. Faces appear beneath them like red and shining fruits.

Two girls, two boys. Four, instead of the three she'd been expecting. And they're only kids, after all.

'We have to walk into an Adviser,' one of them groans.

'Didn't you look where you were going?'

'What, through a giant leaf?'

'You can't see a trailer in the middle of a desert?'

'Nice going,' the smaller of the two boys attacks the other. 'Think you can get us into trouble now? Or can we just go home?'

The older boy adjusts a leaf over him solicitously anyway. 'Keep it straight, OK?'

Above them the sun beats down on the leaves protecting their heads. In an hour they'll be shaking, have headaches; feel obscurely bad all over without knowing exactly why or in which body part.

'Hopefully no immune system damage,' Headingley greets them. 'But hey, you never know.'

'We went to Bayle —' the larger boy starts.

'Name?'

'Bruce Hobhouse Stallingham.'

'Thought so.'

' — and we kind of missed the tunnel.'

Headingley glances up briefly. 'No way out from the Undercliff 'cept a dive off the cliffs into the sea.'

'We're on our way home.' The fairer of two girls squares up to her. 'You've got no right to stop us.'

'I've every right under the sun,' Headingley laconically Advises, 'when you go unProtected.' She indicates the leaves. 'It'll getcha through those, every time.'

'You're out in it,' UltraVi says.

''Case you hadn't noticed.' Headingley taps the awning above her. Behind her, her trailer simmers in the mid-morning heat. 'BluScreen as standard. Ninety-nine point nine per cent protection.'

The girl strips off some Approveds, revealing violet eyes. 'Young for an Adviser, aren't you?'

'Well, you know, I wasn't that smart in school.' The Young Persons Training Package has supplied Headingley with answers to questions like these. 'But I never went out in full sol. You'd know better, of course.'

'I know I can go where I want.'

'Within exposure limits.'

'Which are Advisory.'

'Advisory, of course.' Headingley steps back to invite

them under the awning. 'OK, I'll need your rads. You're officially now under Caution and obliged to be fully Advised. Don't mind Sikes – down! Bark's worse'n his bite.'

With sunburned faces and bleeding hands from the spines of the 'rhubarb' stems, with the inevitable recriminations for going outside and running away already ringing in their ears, the Stallingham boys, Reeve and UltraViolet haul reluctantly into the shade of an SAS-issue trailer that strangely smells of beer.

'We're talking twice your Approved yearly dose.' Headingley whistles over the radiation reading. She runs Vi's rad band through again to check the colour gradation. 'See that? Graph peaks in the danger area. No mistaking that colour. Know what that colour says?'

'But I've hardly been out at all.'

'That colour says forty-two rads. Kiss goodbye to Solstice Day. No going outside for two years.'

'I know what's happened here.' Relief floods in as Vi remembers the last time she took off her rad band. 'What's actually happened here is, I've got about twenty rads, but the reason it looks like more –'

'Here's your meter back.'

'The reason I'm reading so high is –'

'Put it on again.'

'– I held it out in the sun.'

'You put your rad band out in the sun.' Headingley swipes Reeve's band through the thermoluminescent detector, where it glows reassuringly blue. 'And why would you want to do that?'

'To get past Smiley quickly. He sells the *Sol*, corner of Concourse and Hobbes? Always keeps us for ages, and we were late for self-defence –'

'Tell it to Central Advice.' Headingley moves on to Bruce. 'It's out of my hands, in any case. Health Records have you tabbed. You won't get credit to go outside, so say goodbye to Christmas.'

'Maybe you should clean up tunnel-trash instead of measuring rads.'

Headingley turns to face her. 'You don't mean that.'

UltraViolet throws her indignation, her Ki, against Headingley's blunt-nosed officialdom. *I know I don't*, her violet eyes say. *I'm angry you're part of the Service.*

'Unusual, aren't you?' Headingley acknowledges. 'Afraid you risk a Confining Order. They don't like unusual, usually.'

On the return to Condorcet along the cracked ocean boulevard, a rare outing along the shoreline, Vi probes Headingley's life as they're driving along.

'You joined up right after school.'

'Pretty much.'

'So did you have pets at home?'

'Nightjar? He wasn't a pet. A horse won't let you down, the way people will.'

'Hope he wasn't white.'

'Guess again.'

'Black?'

'As night. He hung on longer.'

'I'm sorry.'

'Not as sorry as I was.' The fate of equines everywhere crosses both their minds. Headingley's knuckles are white on the wheel. Leos, they never forget.

'You're a Leo, right?'

'Not going to hit me with that horoscope stuff, are you?'

'I write that stuff on the Net. A million hits a day.'

'You're kidding.'

'Popular site.'

'I guess people like to feel there's a future.'

'It isn't always good news. Horror-scopes, I call 'em.'

Headingley turns a sceptical expression on her.

'Violet Life, the site's called.' Suddenly Vi sees the desert in Headingley's eyes: the Headingley underneath the good-cop, bad-cop pose, uniform stripped away, wandering alone in the desert, wild-eyed, filthy, unkempt. She shuts her eyes to shut out the picture of Headingley.

'You all right?'

'Sun headache.'

'Take a bullet. I get them all the time.' Headingley flips open the glove compartment and pulls out a tube of NeuroGems.

Still the desert in her eyes. A pain analgesics can't fix.

'Thanks, I'm OK,' Vi declines.

In the back with Reeve, the vision of Headingley clings to everything around her: the dog, the smell of beer, the SAS hat on the bunk, swinging mugs in the trailer-kitchen, the crushed pills over the floor ...

When they finally reach the Niles compound, Vi waits for the doors to open. Never tried to alter fate before. This is one time it's worth a shot.

The doors open at last and Sikes jumps heavily out.

Headingley drags him back. 'Sikes. Wait.'

Vi jumps down beside her. Bringing up all her Ki into her chest, projecting it out towards her, she tries to find Headingley's eyes.

'I see something weird in your future. I don't see you staying an Adviser. It has to do with the desert, and whatever it is, it's going to be soon –'

'Like I believe you're psychic.'

'Remember the Nightjar – one white sock, left back leg, am I right?'

Headingley whitens. 'Right.'

'He's under Fulson Meadow. I can see him now.'

Headingley pushes away. Covers her mouth with her hands.

'A dead horse? That's gross,' Reeve says. 'Can't you see you're upsetting her? You'd better go in. I'll call you.'

'So, TV's Doctor Niles.'

'That's me.' Nick saw them coming already.

The tunnel-flap dusts them down as they enter the kitchen. Headingley smiles palely. 'Family not taking your advice, Doctor Niles?'

'Everyone makes their choices. We're not in Boot Camp now.'

'I'm going for a shower.' Vi ducks upstairs.

'How much exposure did she have?'

'Enough.'

'Where were they?'

'The Vale.' Headingley signs the Caution and rips it off her pad. She searches the doctor's face as she hands it over, not unfriendly, just professional. 'Nice place you've got here.'

'You always talk like a TV show?'

'You should know, Doctor Niles.'

The sound of slamming drawers announces Vi's mood upstairs. Headingley wonders briefly what a man like this, with a home like this, does with his time.

'Different, isn't she?'

'Vi's an original, all right.' Nick lets himself smile.

'You know she told me she saw me flip out in the desert? As if I'm going to blow off Full Adviser, with promotion just around the corner.'

'Not much older than she is, are you?' Nick tries to keep it light. 'Vi's premonitions have a way of being self-fulfilling.'

Headingley puts on her hat. 'Self-fulfilling or not, she might want to mind what she's doing. We have to file a report.'

'Of course.'

'They have been fully Advised. This Caution gives you the details. Your daughter has forty rads. Next time it'll be the Centre and a full Confining Order.'

Forty rads. The doctor reels. 'I understand. And thank you.'

*

UltraViolet, showering away the dirt the day outside just threw at you, you can't shower away the memory, the *feel* of the wind on your face! Go downstairs, you'll still feel it. Open and search the fridge. It'll stay with you today, and every day, until you feel it again.

'Nice shower?' The doctor jumps a little as UltraVi enters the kitchen and starts slamming around for food, the towel around her head emphasizing her angular face.

'Fine.'

'What just happened?'

'I opened the fridge.'

Nick slams it shut again. 'What was that about?'

'Freedom, I think.' Vi twirls away with a fridge-frosted plum. 'The right to make your own choices. That would be it.'

'You realize you've absorbed the equivalent of two years' worth of solar radiation?'

'I know it looks as if I have —'

'You must've sunbathed all day to clock up forty rads.'

'Twenty, actually.'

'This is your health we're talking about.'

'Dad, you don't understand.'

'There have to be limits. I guess I should have set some before.'

'I have to set my own.'

'It seems I can't trust you to do that.'

'The problem is to find a form of association —' Vi savours another plum — 'which will defend and protect the individual, and in which each may still obey himself alone, and remain as free as before.'

'Rousseau?'

'Conference notes on your desk.'

'You know there'll be no more conference fees. Not if this gets out.' Nick runs his hands through his hair. 'All I've worked for, Vi. I'm presenting papers on UV exposure, and my own daughter has no sun-manners?'

For some reason Vi flashes on Stevenson Stallingham, his old face, like a younger Nick, his electric air of destiny and action.

'You know it'll go on my record. It might affect my career.'

'So live a little, Dad.'

'They're probably listening now.'

'The Vale, you mean?'

'Who else?'

Under the sunbed bronzing he undergoes every other week, the doc's face is pale and strained. Actually much tenser than he seems, his intelligence goes along with unpredictability, as UltraVi knows very well from memories of the way he used to be. Nick Niles remade himself when he became a UV guru; but today the skin around his eyes looks puffy the eyes themselves troubled and tired.

'What's up, doc?'

'I feel old.'

'Done any vitamins lately?'

Nick fills a glass at the sink and looks at it. Vi cracks a couple of Vit. D tablets out of a tube and hands them one each. 'I embarrassed you, didn't I?'

'And?'

'I went outside.'

'You endangered your health, worst of all.'

'Dad, I told you –'

'My job's telling people to listen to experts. I'm an expert myself.' Nick throws back the D. 'Your mother hears about this, I lose holiday access and we don't see each other all summer. Can I make myself clearer?'

Vi shakes her head.

'OK.'

Later, Vi hangs her head over the bath. The vivarium temporarily positioned inside it smells moist and cool and very slightly fishy. The tiny frogs are hard to see, until you're attuned to their world. Mostly they sit around motionless except for their beating throats, occasionally gulping air, waiting, always waiting, while their tails are consumed into their bodies, fitting them for the world outside. Anytime now they'll be needing live flies instead of bits of bacon.

'Hey, froggies, here's the deal.' Vi props her chin on the edge of the bath. 'The deal is, there's a perfect place, where there's bowls of soup beside the fire and you can go to the beach in the summer whenever you want to.'

Where the rays of the autumn sunshine die before a fire warming Mum and Dad and a dozing dog or cat, a pile of comfy shoes, wellies beside the door …

'A place for you, a place for me … know what this place is called?'

The Undercliff seems so far away now. So much effort to

get there. Why even bother to go outside when SimDream waits in your room?

The girl with the violet eyes gets up and washes her face, pads along the corridor back to her room, goes in and loads SimDream. SimDream software simulates your dreams ... anywhere you want to go.

In no time the rising sun behind the church in Afterminster heralds another perfect day in Violet's bedroom. Wall-high 'parents' bid her goodbye after a cosy breakfast around the range. Bye, Mum! Bye, Dad! On the way to the dreaming spires of a college made of golden stone, a lovely garden beckons across the park.

'Vi!' Nick's voice. 'You Questing?'

Still in SimDream, Vi options Dream Garden. Dream Garden includes a Voice Recognition Facility that builds a garden as you describe it. Remembering a venerable old house she visited once when a child, Vi paints the garden of her dreams in mounting, visionary phrasing:

'I'm walking in a lovely garden decked in green ...'

(Lovely garden surrounds her.)

'... periwinkles twinkle like stars along a path ...'

(Periwinkles pop out like stars.)

'... which brings me to a grave old house.'

(Grave old house appears.)

'Behind it lies a pond filled with those tall yellow flowers that grow in marshes?'

(Yellow Flag jumps up.)

'Tadpoles wriggle in the pond; azaleas and those big showy things – magnolias? – stand guard over a solemn lawn, and everywhere birds sing. And over everything lies a great hush, as though in the church of spring ...'

As though in the church of spring – lovely – did I do that? Vi sits wondering in a lovely garden, and it seems to her that the magnolia petals fall, showering her with creamy blossoms ...

'Vi! You up there?' The shout from downstairs cuts through the garden like winter.

'I can't hear you! Yes!'

'I cut up a frog for cell-tissue today. I meant to ask you, but you weren't here.'

'You cut up one of my frogs?'

'In the interests of science.'

Poor froggie. 'Don't do it again.'

'Chloroformed it first.'

'Don't do it again!'

Vi wanders from Dream Garden back to the Dream Village option, revisiting the autumnal main square in Afterminster once again, with its golden stone buildings and drowsing dog roses, a place where parents don't cut up your pets the minute you go outside ...

There has to be a perfect place somewhere. Somewhere the clouds don't make chlorine. Somewhere the ozone doesn't dissolve, sliding away like a veil to reveal the tender, pulsing heart of something you love very much.

Chapter 8

Hot

The summer crawls slowly around the timeless Niles compound like a shadow around a sundial. Nick bursts out of the house now and then to harvest squash or beans. Snails crisp on paths. Tomatoes ripen and fall. Chives and radish reach up, go to seed under Blu. Reeve passes her Science Two module. Vi toys with homework on the terminal beside her bed, finally exiting her biology project and catching her face in the mirror. *So you have a Caution, so what? What does it mean to be Hot? To have absorbed more rays than you actually wanted or needed, if not as much as they think?*

Entering 'Cosmic Rays' under 'Search by subject', Vi waits to see what'll come up:

Cosmic rays are high-energy subatomic particles that come from the Sun and outer space. Cosmic rays are more intense at **high altitudes,** because they are gradually absorbed by the ozone in the upper atmosphere –

What ozone?

– so aircrews and people living at altitude receive more radiation. The intensity of cosmic rays is about **twenty per cent lower indoors,** because buildings also absorb them.

You're looking at a lot of indoors, girl. UltraVi pages down:

Radiation can affect **DNA** directly by breaking the strands of these molecules. When workers are exposed to radiation, the doses they receive can be measured by **thermoluminescent dosimeters,** which release light in proportion to the radiation dose when they are subsequently heated …

This web site came out of the ark. Do they think people don't realize that workers who go out in the sun have their rads 'adjusted'?

Vi's own rad meter, a function of her wristband, glows an odd shade of pink. Any more rads, it reverts to bright red and triggers an officer at Solar Advice to protect her, despite herself. She could leave it home on the shelf. But then it would signal 'Unused'. No matter where it is, its record is indestructible and wired to the name 'Violet Niles' through social security links. She may or may not try to lose it, but wherever she goes it marks her as Hot: a loner, beyond Advice, probably Monitored, not good to know, someone who fell through the net, like those sad sacks who live on the boulevards, begging for overdates veg.

Hot means no outside credits; no Solstice Day, no Christmas outside, no snow, if snow ever comes.

Not for two entire years.

Vi logs off and drops in the day's violet contacts in the mirror, blinking them in, considering. *So why not turn up at the hospital, throw a fit, insist my rads are checked and the record set straight? But where does that leave Nick? On the front of the 'Sol' with a cheesy grin and a daughter that went outside and barbecued his reputation?*

Hot, she most certainly is. But there has to be a way round it.

'Got the list?' Nick puts his head around the door.

Vi nods, mouth open, blinking.

'Come on, then, let's get it over with.'

'Thought you were doing morning TV.'

'Recorded it yesterday.'

'Oh.'

I didn't know you were gone, Dad. I don't know the things that you do. Two lives, one house. How long would it take for one of them to realize the other had gone for days, maybe even moved out?

The monthly trip to Wesley Co-op later that day convinces UltraViolet that her health score has changed for ever, if she ever doubted it. Sitting like a tremendous bath-bubble in a quarry, the Wesley biomes, or bio-domes, house fully grown tropical trees under their triple-layered skin. Each hexagon making up the skin of the biomes can inflate or deflate in response to ultraviolet conditions. Squatting in its hole under sweeping approach tunnels, it reminds UltraVi of a toad.

Goods come in and out in the covered market. Sometimes a windfall of apples, very occasionally the rare sight of hair conditioner. The only guarantees are the biome vegetables, grown next door under the creaking hexagons of Nacron developed by BluShield Worldwide.

Bumping into Reeve on the market floor strikes Vi as more than a coincidence.

'Thought I'd see you.'

'And you did.'

'I always know when I'll meet people.'

'Self-defence this week?'

'Not sure.'

'You didn't text me.'

'No.'

'How's the Horrors?'

'I let them go.'

'You should start them again.' There's nothing to say. 'See you.'

'Reeve –'

'What?'

I need to make the effort to see you. To say, I want a friend. 'There's gooseberries. In the garden.'

'So call me when they've gone.' Reeve gags, then grins. In moments the crowd swallows her up, and Vi feels the stretching to breaking point of a very real connection. Feeling detached from everything and even a little tearful, she lets herself be buffeted and swept along to an open-fronted shop on the Mall under the name 'Condorcet Druggist'.

Vi picks over a basket of sticky cosmetics next to a stand advertising plants for medicines – mandrake for headaches, John's Wort for Seasonal Affective Disorder, evening primrose for cancer. A leaflet reads: 'Imagine life without plants. No wood. No cloth. No flowers. No food. Just an empty room to sit in. BluShield brings you Nacron. The future of sustainable living.' Cameras set in the centres of the hexagons overhead have picked out Violet Niles as an outcast already, though she doesn't yet know it. But at the pharmaceuticals checkout, there's trouble over Spinach Moisturiser.

'Sorry. No recognition.'

'What, my card's expired?'

'Card not valid.' The checkout hands it back.

'Why not?'

'You're not in the system.'

The Spinach Moisturiser waiting at the till looks more desirable than ever. A Skin Tonic to Revitalise Sun Damaged Skin. There would be some stupid mistake. Vi crossly finds Nick.

'Dad, can I borrow a credit card?'

'Sure, lost your own?'

'Not recognized. I don't know.'

She hurries back. Presents it. But the assistant returns Nick's card too.

'Sorry, no recognition.'

'But this one must be valid.'

'System doesn't recognize the card.'

'Must be a mistake.'

'Sorry about that. Next.'

As though being out of the system were catching, Vi senses the queue at the checkout distancing itself from her and her problem credit. No systems recognition. Happens all the time. Especially when you're Hot.

Recrossing the Minster Mall buffeted by shoppers and shoppers' bags full of items no longer available to her, wondering why everything looks so different now she's excluded from it, Vi catches sight of her reflection sliding from hexagon to hexagon along the length of the main Wesley biome – and a glint from above. What, cameras in the roof? Vi looks them square in the eye. *Don't care if you think I'm Hot. You think Hot describes me?*

Tracking Nick down by the sound of his voice isn't hard, so much as embarrassing.

'What d'you mean, not recognized? Lemme see that machine.'

'Niles, N. A., Credit Denied,' the man with the *Wesley* lapel badge tries to explain.

'I want to see the manager –'

'I *am* the manager. Your card isn't recognized. I'm sorry.'

'Since when?'

'I'm afraid I can't disclose.'

'You can't tell me when my credit was cancelled? I'm Nick Niles, Doctor Nick Niles. You may have seen me on television.'

'It's a Recent Refusal,' The manager tabs a few keys. 'Anyone been outside?'

'Hi.' Vi appears.

'All right,' the doc says tightly. 'Give me back my card.'

'Why don't you try Central Banking to clear up any mistake?'

'Yeah, why don't I?' Nick stuffs away his plastic. 'Central banking. Why not? That would be just dandy.'

Over chicory coffee in the Minster Mall, Nick's indignation rises. 'A piffling Caution from a teenage Adviser, and we're out of the system? Wait till I get hold of Ed Gowan from Central Advice –'

'Dad. I went out. People like us don't realize. Once you're out of the system, it's hard to get back in.'

'So what do we do for food?' the doc asks dangerously.

'I suppose they'll sort it out. They can't exclude you as well.'

Can they?

Suddenly the Minster Mall looks anything but friendly, its crumby Village Square of grey and yellow plastics about as homely as the plastic arches of the 'church' over the Tea & Coffee counter.

An empty packet bowls over the floor in the thick, warm breeze from the tunnel-mouths opening on to the Mall from Hobbes, from Locke Junction, from all points north to Condorcet. Vi feels like letting the tunnel-breath blow over her and claim her, free to go with the wind, no difficult decisions, like the packet bowling over the floor.

For a moment, just for a moment, she knows how the tunnel-rats feel. Tunnel-rats, they call them, strung out on Seatonal, a feel-good prescribed for indoor blues before it became a problem. Tunnel-rats with filthy broken nails and a sign saying, 'Sun Struck and Homeless. Please Help.'

Vi shivers. There, but for – 'I hate it here. Let's go.'

Recrossing the biome to the Anderville tunnels, Vi feels a Jope-like moment. Sure enough, there's Danny.

'My cards got cancelled, can you believe that?' Vi shoots at him impatiently.

Jope stares at her under the mahoganies imported when Brazil had a rain forest.

'They actually stopped my credit … hello?'

Jope stirs. 'You Hot?'

'Warmish.'

'So what did you think?'

'Didn't know this would happen.'

'Oh, yeah,' Jope says sagely. 'And there's other stuff.'

'So what do we do for food?'

'Barter. Beg. Borrow. Re-evaluation can take for ever.'

'You know a lot.'

'My brother's out.'

'Didn't know you had a brother.'

'Daley ran out three years ago.'

'How old is he?'

'Seventeen.'

'How come –'

'We never talk about him. So that's why you wouldn't know.'

UltraVi pictures Daley Jope, an older Danny, out beyond the biomes, where salt-brush and certain spruces are the only things resisting UV-B.

A vein ticks in Jope's neck. 'Hear about Stallingham?'

'Which one?'

'Stevie's in hospital.'

'Since when?'

'Since for ever.'

Reeve appears at Vi's elbow. 'Stevie's in hospital?'

'Intensive care,' Jope confirms.

'Stevie's in danger of dying?'

'Some virus. He went outside.'

'But – that was ages ago.'

'So?'

Vi flushes. 'No one told me.'

'So text more.'

'You could text *me*.'

Never has isolation in the house seemed a more horrible trap. Tragedy, things she should know, out there – Why had no one said?

You won't get away with it, the Adviser had Advised them, that morning out under the rhubarb leaves in the middle of the baking desert. Hopefully no immune system damage, but hey, you never know. The Adviser had tapped the awning above her. Pointed out that leaves were no protection – but still, a virus …

'I didn't know either,' Reeve says softly. 'We should stay in touch more.'

A million chaotic impressions of the Undercliff fill the moment, the sun lancing down through the trees, Stevie out on The Beak; shouting to him, Come Back! His answer against the sea-haze, I'm not coming back! I told you! His future, obscure but important, his face looming larger, more fully –

'Ready to go now? Vi?'

Vi comes to. 'Dad.'

'Something happened? What is it?'

'Going to Bruce's.'

'Now?'

Vi nods, backing away.

'You won't go outside?'

'I promise.'

Promises made on shaky ground tend to shift with the ground they were made on. Vi looks back once before the dim lights of the tunnels extinguish the bustle of Wesley, to see the doc, slack-mouthed and astonished, under ferns advertising Wonder Anti-Virals Soon To Be Extracted from their stems, and knows that he has as much of a clue about her life as she guesses she has about his ...

The tunnels between Wesley and Sepulveda moan with the gale outside blustering over the desert. The conversation with Bruce is at least as stormy, as Reeve and Vi take the Brankshire East tunnel and burst in on the Stallingham kitchen, where a bowl rocks in the sink, as though recently discarded.

Vi feels the kettle. Warm.

'Bruce! You there?'

Bruce appears like a ghost. *Stevie.* Did someone say it?

Vi searches his face. 'He's going to be all right.'

Bruce looks at Vi wordlessly.

'He *so* has things to do with his life –'

'It's an infection, they think.' Bruce's voice is rusty. 'Some virus he got from outside.'

'Bad?'

Bruce nods.

'So when will they know?'

'His airway swelled up last night. "Poor but stable" this morning. He was getting better, then the medicine –' Bruce swallows. 'They don't say "Poor" unless it's bad, unless ... you know, they ...'

'And you're here on your own?

'They sent an Adviser.'

Great. 'Where is she?'

'He. The living room. Go in if you want; I don't mind.'

Vi and Reeve enter a rug-filled saloon hung with Bruce's mother's paintings. Bruce's step-mother isn't in. She went to the hospital with his father, Bruce says, but he doubts they'll let her see Steve. Blood relations are quarantined, step-relatives not encouraged. It's why he isn't there himself. As few as possible Exposures.

'Exposures?'

'People with close contact.' The Adviser rises and smiles.

Vi steps back. 'Smiley.'

'Davis,' he introduces himself. 'They call me Smiley in the tunnels, you know.'

'You're an Adviser now?'

'Didn't you say, "Get a job"?'

'Did I say that?'

'Sometimes. The girl with the violet eyes.' He smiles into them, remembering her, from the other side of that invisible line she crossed when she went outside. 'I'm making Adviser, no problem. They say I have a friendly face.'

But the Sol used to rubbish Advisers. 'Aren't you selling out?'

'I work from the inside now. A bit of the Trojan Horse.' Impossible to understand what he means. 'Now I come to Bruce about his brother.'

His brother. Yes.

'Anyone like some vegetable juice?' Bruce Hobhouse Stallingham sweats over the strain of entertaining three visitors. 'I'm sorry I haven't peeled them, but – anyone like a carrot?'

'I'm going to the hospital,' Vi decides later. 'I don't believe what they say.'

'You're Hot, remember?' Reeve points out.

'But I'm not really Hot, I left my rad band out in the sun.'

'We could clock it,' Smiley suggests.

'Clock it?'

Smiley puts out his hand for it. 'Correct it. Show you how.'

Producing a black dosimeter, he slots Vi's rad band into it.

'We're measuring solar radiation by thermoluminescence, represented by visible colour. When the rad band is heated, light is released in proportion to the dose. When cooled, the reverse is occurring.'

Vi watches, bemused. 'But you're an Adviser.'

Smiley hands back the rad band, now blue. 'I left you eight rads. You're cool.'

'Why are you doing this?'

'Your reading was incorrect.'

'Will you stop me from going outside?'

'Only if Unprotected.'

Vi meets Smiley's eyes. The understanding between them would be complete, if only Bruce weren't in the way.

'*My* brother. I want to go.'

'Can't let you do that, Bruce.' Smiley's smile means No.

'Coming?' Vi means Reeve. 'Make sure he isn't Confined?'

'Call you.' Reeve comforts Brucie.

Smiley texts rapidly on his wrist-display: **Hospital on Ventura. Go by Glade. Take these.**

'For us? Are you sure?'

Smiley puts his finger to his lips. 'Reeve Dunkley and Violet Niles – take my advice, go now.'

Shaking the protective suits out of their Solar Survival packs at the first junction on Brankshire East, Reeve and Vi take stock.

'I can't believe he gave us these.'

'Shades, sunblock, compass –' Reeve meets UltraVi's eyes – 'Why would he give us this stuff unless he *wanted* us to go outside?'

'Safely,' Vi reminds her. 'We were going anyway.'

'You trust him?'

'No way – do you?'

Reeve fiddles with a zip. Shakes out the legs of a suit.

'I can go by myself, you know,' Vi says. 'I don't need you to come. Just because Stevie got ill on the Undercliff –'

'*I* made us come back in full sol.'

'No one made him run out.'

'U V probably weakened his immune system so he got a virus.'

'You don't know that for sure.'

Reeve climbs heavily into a rustling close-weave suit in yellow and purple Solar Advisory Service colours. 'I thought they were green this year – what's the date on yours?'

UltraVi checks her suit. '*Use by* 2016. I was eleven then.'

How much has changed since then? 2016. The year dad blew it. When Grace smashed all the alcohol in the house and packed up her bags and left. Above Condorcet and neighbouring Bayle, where Grace, Vi's mother, now lives, the gale whistles and rushes around the globe, with few cloud systems to slow it.

Far into the dimly lit distances, the tunnels shudder and moan.

Shaking out a suit more sun-proof, by far, than the one she cut out on her bedroom floor in a fit of improvisation, Vi draws on both legs and takes her life in her hands.

This isn't about a runaway boy, maybe ill or Confined. This is about inside and outside. The right to come and go. A sustainable way to behave. Solutions, where everything is compromised. Everything under the sun.

Still, she didn't see herself being quite so brave and decisive.

'It's funny I didn't see it.'

'What?'

'You. Me. This.' UltraViolet, setting out to an Isolation Hospital in the middle of a virus-friendly environment that may almost have killed him, to visit a boy she may have helped put there! 'I didn't see it coming. I didn't see any of this.'

Chapter 9

Good Morning with— Doctor Niles

'Hello and good morning. On "Sun Spots" this morning we ask, is *QuestHolme* taking over our lives?' The television presenter's name is Rowena Giles. Her brittle smile never betrays the fact that she has few friends. 'If *you* have to escape from the Castle Gorm to get your breakfast, or if you have a youngster upstairs you haven't seen in three days, you might want to listen to this. But first today's weather from Diane.'

'Sun, sun and more sun, I'm afraid.' Today Diane wears a purple pin in her lapel. 'As you can see, my solar-cell sun-badge is violet today, which means we're in for maximum UV-B, and the outlook is pretty sunny, I'm afraid, towards the end of the week —'

Right now rain is off the map. So is any change. Diane gives a few frightening rad projections and brings up the Solar Flares Diary, pictures from some wandering space telescope showing stupendous gouts of flame spurting from the surface of the sun.

'Solar activity quite intense today, so some electromagnetic interference can be expected. Nothing to worry about too much, though flares at this time of year can be unpredictable and they *can* cause a blip on computers, so back up that data, won't you? That's it from me. Rowena?'

'And now the effects of addictive games.' Rowena Giles's stiff hair turns to camera a second or two after her face. 'Do games like *QuestHolme* contribute to a condition some commentators are calling Bedroom Fixated Teens? A recent report in *World Health* suggests that many of today's youngsters are spending as much as seventy per cent of their time in electronic environments, instead of making social contact. Is staying in turning young people into recluses? Jenny Lind asked Doctor Nick Niles, a leading consultant on the effects of ultraviolet radiation.'

The scene switches. Jenny Lind smiles. ' Doctor Niles ...'

'Hello.'

'Health effects of staying indoors?'

'Of course, you must keep up your Vitamin-D,' Nick opens cautiously over his blue-grey suit, his old surfie hair slicked back.

'But no contact with other people – is this an effect of UV culture? The thin end, perhaps, of what we might call "isolationism"?'

'It's certainly true that a large percentage of young people are choosing cyber experience over real life.' Nick tries a craggy smile. 'But this could represent a challenge.'

'Can Questing for days on end be healthy?'

'We need to redefine healthy. If staying out of UV-B means creating alternative stimuli indoors, so long as it isn't carried to excess then, yes, I think it can be healthy.'

'How would you define excess?'

'Excess means different things for different people. The same people you find Questing for many hours at a time are probably the ones you're going to find indulging in any outdoor activity to excess.'

'You mean boys.'

'QuestHolme appeals to everyone. And, you know, it isn't all bad. Studies have shown that clue-solving games like QuestHolme equal On-line College Modules for mental stimulation.'

'But social skills must suffer.'

'New skills can develop, imagination especially.'

'But doesn't this send a grim message to parents – that children would rather Quest, even when winter comes?'

'QuestHeads have to come out when they're ready. I guarantee that trying to limit them will increase the desire to Quest.'

'You wouldn't limit your own child?'

'My daughter Quests all the time.'

'So no need for any concern?'

'Anti-social behaviour is always a concern, but this can be an effect of Seasonal Affective Disorder. Parents will find that this passes on Solstice Day.'

'And if it doesn't?'

'Some loners may need help. But these are a small percentage.'

'Any advice for Solstice Day?'

'BluShield have come up with these Smart Shades.' The doc slips on a pair of sunglasses. 'Most sunglasses fool the body by telling it there's no UV. These will change colour in winter sunshine to tell you when you've had enough.' He slips a pair over Jenny's nose. 'My daughter tells me they're brisk.'

'Smart Shades, what next?' Jenny removes them immediately and switches to video link. 'Solar Advisor Bonnie Headingley has a word about winter sunshine. Miss Headingley …'

'Bo.' Headingley flickers on screen, the posters behind her placing her at Central Advice.

'Can you reassure us that this year we'll get three full months outside?'

'Probably two, I'm afraid.' Bo's eyes look hunted.

'Surely, from December –'

'December looks shaky right now.'

'But aren't we predicted more cloud-cover this winter?'

'Clouds aren't necessarily good. Those low-lying clouds may look beautiful, but they're destroying stratospheric ozone. Complex chemical reaction involving chlorines. We could be looking at rolling those tunnels up late this year.' *Hi, doc,* Headingley's gaze seems to say. *I could make things pretty Hot for you, Doctor UV, with your daughter who went outside.*

'Are you saying we can expect Christmas indoors?'

Headingley blinks. 'Depends.'

'Could be a normal winter.' Nick Niles to the rescue. 'That ozone hole could shift.'

'But it never disappears completely, does it?'

'We Advise everyone to be careful, whatever the weather. Don't forget the Cosmic Ray Code ...' Headingley passes her hand over her eyes. 'I'm sorry, I'm a little sun-sick.'

'And there we must leave it, I'm afraid.' Jenny turns to Nick. 'Nick, what advice would you give to a parent whose child refuses to log off at any time ...'

Stevie turns off the telly.

Before he can turn on to his side he has to rearrange his drips and be careful not to lie on the tubes. The intensive bed in Virus Decontamination monitors his every move; the hospital folds its silence around him like a soft and muffling blanket.

Outside some bird may be singing, but the boy in the bed wouldn't know. Further from a natural way of living than he's ever been in his life, isolated and slightly jaundiced, Stevenson Stallingham's immune system attempts to recover from the anti-viral drugs pumped into his body. Nothing seems to penetrate the stillness of the isolation hospital. Friends may come and friends may go ... but dads are always waiting outside. In his case, staying in the Guest Unit while recovery takes place.

So he had a crisis last night. The doctors here don't know why his immune system has let in a virus that gives him swollen airways, but they've got it under control by trying every med under the sun. Unfortunately he reacted to the anti-virus, and it's been touch and go for a while, but steroids have saved the situation, and his response has been 'dramatic'.

'An allergic response to the environment.' That's the official report. The Consultant went through his charts today, showed medical students his chest, gave him a plastic Seshwan and a comic, told him he had a lucky face. The plastic Emperor Seshwan stands beside the comic on Stevie's beside table, reminding him at every turn of Questgames he hasn't played. He asked for *QuestHolme* already, but they humm'd and hah'd and said No. They haven't a clue why his defences are down, as though he had aged thirty years. He hasn't told them he's been outside. No one cross-checked with Central Advice. Stevie seems young for a Leaker. Best guess is contact with animals in fruit. A tarantula in a 'hand' of bananas sent to a local biome, and bob's your uncle, an imported virus. This virus is named KV8. First seen in frogs in Savannah.

Stevie dozes between sleeping and waking, while overhead monitors bleep and tubes lie crushed under his outflung arm, his hand flexing quietly as he dreams of the Undercliff, his uptilted fingers as big as the characters in the comic magnified through the glass of water beside his bed, their speech bubbles magnified too: 'braD I DIDN'T THink you'd come.'

As Stevie sleeps, a single white flower from a wood half a kilometre away is slipped softly into the glass, blocking out bits of the speech bubbles reflected through the water: braD I DIDN'T — *stem of flower* — THink you'd come.

Chapter 10
Exceptional Flares——

Tubes and monitors.

Drips and a table loaded with medication. A computer log at the foot of his bed, showing that the crisis has passed, the only good news in a pretty depressing scenario. Poor Stevie. Only a pathetic comic beside his bed and a plastic Emperor Seshwan to show that the person in bed 306 isn't a crippled old man.

UltraViolet adjusts the slightly crushed flower she carried all this way for him, so that it stands to attention in its glass of water: a single white harebell, the only natural thing in three wards, not including Stevie and herself. Probably she shouldn't have brought it. Who knows what germs it might bring in from outside? Still, its fresh and starry presence brings a breath of the woods into the sterile air, worth it for the first thing Stevie might notice in the moment he opens his eyes.

Look and feel like a doctor, Vi reminds herself. The SAS suit got her through the security beams outside, mainly because its texture failed to trigger alarms. But only stealth and nerve were going to bring her inside. Not for nothing had she watched endless re-runs of Emergency Alert ...

I could be a doctor, I could be a doctor, they don't know that I'm not a doctor ...

An impulse had led her to whip the white coat from the back of a staff-room door on entering hospital reception. Confidence had carried her along the corridors of the hospital; had empowered her to search for Intensive Care.

Now this. Stevenson Stallingham, who ran wild on the Undercliff, brave, decisive, free, now hitched to a hospital monitor. His face looks unlike the Stevie she knows, without his personality behind it. Empty, slack – not Stevie. Wake up, wake up, wake up. He could be thirteen or thirty.

'Stevie – can you hear me?'

Optioning 'Status' on the terminal at the end of the bed, Vi sees that his condition has improved from 'Stable' to 'Comfortable' in the course of the last three hours. This is encouraging, after all. 'Allergic response to environment now controlled by super-histamine,' say his Notes. Now controlled. Not out of control. So a little fresh air won't kill him.

'Stevie –'

What? She wants to see him sit up. Get out of bed, turn at the door: What are we waiting for? No use projecting things that aren't there. Instead his body lies motionless.

'So you're really ill, not Confined.' UltraVi touches his hand. 'Reeve wanted to be here too, but she twisted her ankle, guess where? The Glade. That's where I got the flower, hope you like it.' *Please wake up. It doesn't end here. So many things we have to do.*

The white flower stands in its glass like a star of hope beside him. He looks so like Brucie lying there, so very like a crushed flower himself. Maybe he's contagious. Maybe she shouldn't get close.

Vi puts on the telly, turns down a weather report.

'A report just in of exceptional flares – '

She flicks around the channels, but ten of them are dead. Even the weather report just died. Exceptional flares aren't trousers, but sometimes she wishes they were.

'What's on?'

Vi spins around. 'You're awake!'

'Always.'

'You mean . . . Did you just hear what I said?'

'Violet.' Stevie opens his eyes. 'Do you like your name?'

'Hate it.'

'That's what I thought.' He grins. 'Why did you come?'

'Get you out, if you want.'

'Why?'

'One, Reeve 'n' me felt responsible. Two, you might be Confined. Three –' UltraViolet sees Stevie's face on a wall. Larger, on the side of a building. An important face, saying strange things, whispering hidden messages – 'there's something we have to do.'

'I've been ready for ages. Let's go.'

Shaky but determined, Steve swings his legs out of bed. Only one problem among many shoots out like a solar flare. It might seem so obvious, it's silly. Stevie's rustling green hospital pyjamas stand between him and freedom. Vi searches lockers vainly. How to get him out with no clothes?

In the desert within sight of the hospital, Bo Headingley wanders on patrol. No point in checking hospital limits. That net of alarm beams takes care of it. Should keep an eye on the area surrounding the hospital. How many times do patients break out? Now and then, maybe. Once in a blue moon – and what if they do? Headingley tries to remember what she's doing, why she should be there in a stiff blue uniform. If they want to go, why not let 'em? Because, she reminds herself with an effort, they could be carrying a virus.

Like the Nightjar. He was infected. Weakened by the sun, so his hide began to bloom with bacterial infestations. He looked like a log covered in lichens by the end, as his gleaming black hide broke down. Kinder to put him to sleep. Bury him deep in the Fulson Meadow, where ragged flowers still bloom.

Thank you, Violet Niles. As if Fulson Meadow weren't already a regular point on a patrol that's going to remind me, every day, of a gleaming black horse I once lost. More than a horse, a friend.

Thank you, Violet Niles, for bringing him before me, so that the memory of the Nightjar visits me in my dreams … I'd put him away, till you brought him out. Showed me what he meant to me.

'So what pet did you have? Did you have any pets at home?'

'Nightjar? He wasn't a pet.'

'What was he, a friend?'

'Of course. A horse won't let you down the way people will.'

'Nightjar — I hope he wasn't —'

'Black as the pit of hell.'

'I'm sorry.'

'Yeah, me too.'

Now the Nightjar sleeps under the place where she rode him so often, one white sock, left back leg, flashing as he stepped out. Headingley revisits him now and again. Lately, she goes every day. The other night, she slept out on his grave. When she woke up, the sun had baked her. Her teeth chattered. Her temperature rose. She saw things in the night.

It was then that the Nightjar began to visit her, appearing out of the heat-haze, growing more solid as she watched for him, muscles rippling, breath jolting out with the rhythm of his evenly paced limbs. Again she can practically feel him. The rippling coat of the Nightjar, curried until it shone; the gathering power in his body, as they took a jump full on; the warmth of his breath on her hands when the day's jumping was done; the apple they shared together before she turned for home. The feel, the smell, the touch of him, when horses were ready for riding, and there were fields to ride them in.

White animals had felt it first. Then black animals began to feel the sun keenly, as their skin absorbed more heat. By the time Headingley was nine, the days when she and Jazzie galloped across open ground together were gone and almost forgotten, and one day the vet came around.

Rory Morrison, his name was. Local equine veterinarian. Putting down animals that were black. They succumbed fast after sun-block failed to save the greys, which were either culled or brought in. Blacks absorbed solar radiation fast. No way could they stay outside, with deadly MVNA Virus racing from field to field, outpacing measures to stop it by an average of two kilometres a day. In the wake of UV-induced changes to DNA, blacks would be sterile anyway.

So Bo had said goodbye to the Nightjar, and to all black horses like him. Except for breeds protected on studfarms, black horseflesh of any kind was yesterday's day at the races.

She'd shut him away until now, Nightjar the proud, the amazing. Until the Niles girl had brought him back with that strange conversation. I *see you out on your own … it has to do with the desert …*

She'd tried to shut her up.

But still the Niles girl had talked on, those insightful violet eyes insinuating themselves into her life, her memories, her dreams; hitting home with a sureness of touch that stripped away her uniform, left her nine again, in the moment Rory Morrison told her: 'All done. He's gone to sleep.'

He hadn't gone to sleep at all.

Her father had tethered the Nightjar's head, because he couldn't afford to stable and keep him indoors. Morrison had felled him with a gun, had washed his hands, hosed down the floor, moved on to the next horse that day.

She'd wanted to plant a tree on the fresh mound of earth

in Fulson Meadow, until her father had told her no point, it would only die. Like the daisies on Sepulveda Drive, the ocean boulevard that had flashed by as she drove four Leakers – two boys, two girls, home that afternoon, weeks ago – was it? – when the Nightjar still slept in his grave instead of whinnying every night beside the trailer.

One night she woke with sound of thunder in her ears – wild horses! Circling the trailer! Suppose Jazzie were one of them? Parting the curtains, the night seemed filled with gleaming backs, the promise of his return. In the morning, criss-cross tracks in the sand confirmed the wild horses, probably thin and diseased, but not her dreams of the Nightjar. She couldn't get it out of her mind.

And still Violet Niles had talked on. 'Mum says, Count me out when there's no trees or fields. I mean, what else is left?'

'Where is she?'

'Over at Bayle. I stay between her and Nick.'

'You OK with that?'

'Have to be. But sometimes …'

'What?'

'I think the mothers go somewhere? A perfect place, and the stove's lit, and the kitchen's bright, and there's cats and dads in front of the fire, and beach towels everywhere in the summer?'

'A fantasy place.'

'Do you Quest?'

'SimDream sometimes.'

'Me too.'

'If I simulated my life,' Headingley remembered finishing

grimly, 'I'd deal myself a better hand. So here we are — everyone out.' Then, as she'd opened the trailer door, the Niles girl had gripped her with her eyes: *You're not going to stay an Adviser. I see you doing something weird. You're going to do it soon.*

She'd tried to shrug it off.

But the Niles girl had played on her mind. It may have been the sunstroke. Next morning saw Headingley sleeping on Jazzie's grave. The next night her temperature had soared. The pots and pans under her bunk clattered as she shook. In the morning she woke under piles of clothing she'd dragged over herself in her sleep. Since then, the Nightjar had haunted her dreams. Days she lay, shivering and sweating, hearing his hooves scrape the trailer, while the gale rattled bushes outside.

Then came the call from the Network. A Channel Seven researcher named Anna Flood. She worked for Grace Evans. Yes. They needed a Solar Adviser to comment on winter sunshine — would she like to contribute to today's discussion? Feeling quite strange, she'd gone into Central Advice and recorded some kind of interview by video-link.

Now Control page her every morning. This morning she was awake.

'Solar Adviser 302238. Your patrol today is Area Nine, the isolation hospital as far as the Glade. Headingley, you used up your leave this year. Get out or get demoted.'

Patrolling hospital limits this morning, Headingley's brain hurts. The low-lying group of buildings that is the isolation hospital swims in the heat-haze. Away under the bluff to the right, the first place patients make for, and the only shade for miles, lies the Glade of spruce trees resistant to ultraviolet radiation.

By lunch-time, the headache's worse.

Headingley sits on a rock, empties her coffee cup over the sand and pulls down her BluScreen visor. After a while a dot near the horizon seems to thicken into a horse-shape. And through the heat-haze, silhouetted against the sky, she sees the Nightjar, switching his tail, waiting for her to join him. He begins to canter, feet flashing, haunches swinging, dark flanks rippling in the sunshine.

'Jazzie, wait for me!' Headingley slips off her helmet to call him, so that ninety-nine per cent UV-B beats down on her unprotected head. The old name slips out so easily, as easy as the swing of Nightjar's stride, stopping, looking back at her, waiting for her to follow ... 'Jazzie, wait for me ...'

He looks like a horse if you're Sun Struck. But in fact it's only Sikesie, dutifully patrolling Area Nine, even if his Adviser isn't. Sikesie, firmly on the scent of Leakers, stopping, looking back, waiting for Headingley to follow him, to wake up and do her job, a big black dog not much like a horse, even from a distance, unless you happen to be sun-crazed.

Sikes, following his nose.

Looking back.

Turning and waiting for Headingley.

Leading her into the Glade.

*

The Glade of partly UV-resistant spruces lies in a fold of the hills, where stone was once quarried for gravel, when roads and gravel were needed. As Headingley deludedly follows her dog, one dot behind another, two more dots begin their journey to the Glade inside a Hospital vehicle – Stevie and Vi, bobbing along, patient and 'doctor', successful so far in conning their way off the premises. Just the checkout at the gate, then a lift to town and freedom. Home, the Quest, or telly ...

'Looks like he's going to examine them.'

'What?'

'Passes, what do you think?' Stevie shrinks down in his seat as the hospital bus, filled with discharged patients, comes slowly to a halt at the last gate between himself, Vi, and freedom, where a hospital security guard waits to let them out.

Beyond hospital limits, Headingley wanders vaguely in search of a horse that has disappeared, a small dot on the desert following another, both of them nearing the Glade.

Under the gloom of the spruces deep in the Glade, a figure turns over stiffly – Reeve with a badly sprained ankle, checking her watch for the millionth time to see if it's still going. Can it take so long to visit a hospital not half a kilometre away? Vi said she wouldn't be long – see Stevie, check that he's ill, not Confined. Back in an hour or two. How can she have been gone for more than four?

Her own fault for falling over. They could have been there and back in the time she's lain here, useless. Twist your ankle like the woman in a frilly dress in some cheesy old

Western, why don't you? She saw the thought in Vi's eyes, as she sat down feeling sick.

'All right?'

'My foot just went way over.' Reeve thought she'd faint for a moment.

Vi had appraised it coolly. After they examined the ankle, 'Better stay here,' Vi had said.

'By myself?'

'I'll go alone. Won't be long.'

Long enough, as it turns out. Something Vi had had to do alone all along, maybe. Maybe she'd just tagged along.

Now this had to happen.

Thank God for the shade — and so peaceful! Reeve looks up, where the tree-tops wag and whisper to one another, a faraway swell, like the sea, sending Chinese whispers around the Glade, variations on the same rushing theme: rish — rush — swash. A squirrel pops out. Reeve and the squirrel look at one another. Then it runs up a tree.

Back before you know it, Vi had said. Fix you up with a bandage I get from the hospital. Stevie'll show me where. He can't be so bad or they'd ring.

Back in no time. Can't be so bad. A bandage from the hospital. Reeve takes off her sock. The swelling's bad all right, but so long as she leaves it alone it doesn't hurt. With her ankle braced with a bandage, she might be able to hobble. But first it needs to get here. Lost on a bluff west of Condorcet, and still so far from home!

Shifting slightly so that the distant Isolation Hospital is framed in the only slit of light between the gloomy rows of trees, Reeve settles down to spot the first sign of rescue. Is that distant dot a figure or a rock? Reeve takes a pull from a bottle of cranberry juice in her bag. Hasn't moved in two minutes. Has to be a rock.

Propping the bottle of juice beside her, folding her arms, leaning against a tree that handily prickles her back to keep her awake, Reeve fixes her gaze determinedly on the complex of low buildings beneath her on the desert floor, as a woodpecker whirrs overhead...

Some time later Reeve opens her eyes. The trees look funny until she straightens, wipes drool from her mouth, spots a big black something padding through the gloom.

Reeve sits up, fully awake. A black dog! Free and unusual!

'Here, then.' Unable to raise herself higher, Reeve strains to make out its shape. 'You're a long way from home.'

The dog sits; sniffs the air; howls a lonely howl:

Arooo—looo—arooooh!

It echoes around the pines.

Reeve shudders. 'Don't – no need to make that noise.'

It tilts its head to listen.

'Here, then. Good boy. Come on.'

Its tail beats on the spruce needles.

'That's it – yes – you're all right.'

The black dog staggers towards her; smells her hand; bows its head.

'Who do you belong to?' The dog's eyes are clouded with

cataracts, Reeve sees now, as she scratches between his ears. 'You must be the howler in the tunnels. Have you been following us? The sun hurt your eyes, did it? That UV makes the lenses opaque. No wonder you're howling, poor thing! I hurt my leg, yes, and you –' She passes her hand in front of his eyes – 'you can't see a thing, can you?'

A blind dog and a lame girl. The howler in the tunnels leans against Reeve and fixes his milky gaze somewhere above her left shoulder. Above them the sun browns the spruce needles and crisps the roof of the Glade, throwing down enough ultraviolet to slowly blind any animal out in it for any length of time.

'What'll Vi say when we tell her?'

Aroo–roo–roooah!

'Yes, but we don't do that now. No more howling in the tunnels. She'll be back soon, through that gap in the trees – oh, well, you can't see it. I keep forgetting, blind as a bat, aren't you?'

Mirabeau County Health Services in Partnership with BluShield Worldwide, the sign over the hospital gate announces.

Vi and Stevie shrink as the guard enters the hospital bus. Vi finds a book of passes in her 'doctor's' coat.

He takes their passes smilingly. 'Wrong colour, wrong day.'

'I'm Doctor Smith.' UltraViolet draws herself up. 'Doctor Niles discharged my patient –'

'Thursday's purple, OK?' He hands the passes back to her.

'Any more Discharges now?' He climbs down. Waves them on. *Thursday's purple, OK?*

Unbelievably, the hospital gates open and the Authorized Carrier drives out along a cracked and little-used highway, once the Mirabeau Turnpike.

Vi hugs herself in the back. She did it, she actually did it! Something so tense and difficult, it would have scored high in the Quest. Yet it had come to her so simply. The key to smuggling Stevie out without everyday clothes was to leave him in hospital PJ's and front it out. Touch and go, but they made it so far. A confident manner helps.

Then the driver asks them, 'Where to?'

'Thoreau Place,' Vi insists.

'What did you say that for?' Stevie hisses.

'Reeve,' Vi explains, 'then home.'

She smiles at the other three patients discharged that morning. They didn't expect to have a doctor with them. So young, these days. Practically a teenager. Her presence is reassuring.

'But Thoreau's in the middle of nowhere.'

'They're not going to drop us at the Glade,' Vi says, between her teeth. 'Reeve first. Then home. That's the bonus points decision.'

The hospital carrier rattles over cracks in the road, throwing them together and apart, jolting the other Releases. At last the driver pulls up in front of a bullet-riddled sign.

Thoreau Compound
The wild, not less than the good

'Here's fine,' Vi says sharply.

The driver throws opens the doors. 'You being met?'

'Any minute.'

'He meant to go home dressed like that?'

'He becomes stressed if pressured. Doctor Niles signed everything out.'

The driver looks at them hard for a moment. Then he bangs up the doors, climbs in and drives away.

'Stressed if pressured,' Stevie says.

'I knew all that stuff I learned on *Emergency Alert* would come in handy sometime.'

Amazing what a uniform can do. They hadn't had the right colour badges or discharge papers. But still they'd been Released. The dust raised by the departing hospital bus has barely settled over the track to Thoreau Place, a crumbling old mansion by a pond dimly visible through failing trees, before UltraVi is anxious to leave it. Reeve, alone on a hill. Reeve, alone in the trees. Reeve, Reeve, *Reeve*.

'The Glade's over there, by the bluff.'

Stevie shades his eyes. 'Sure it's far enough?'

'Shouldn't take us long.' Vi eyes the outlines of what have to be Unauthorized vehicles dotted around Thoreau. 'If we were Questing, we'd steal a car, get there really fast –'

'Get detained, lose Questkeys.'

Vi shrugs a bag off her back. 'You have the jacket, I'll go with the trousers.'

Stevie pulls out the paper-thin Solar Suit. 'You have it. I'm all right.'

'At least put on the hood.'

Vi packs away her 'doctor's' coat, pulls on the yellow and purple jacket. 'If we were Questing now, we could leap levels, get Reeve —'

Stevie looks out from under his Protective hood. 'Get a grip! This is real.'

That sly way he has of getting the upper hand, of always knowing *what to do* ...

'I just got you out of a high-security hospital.'

'All in a day's work.'

'What do you mean?'

'You're Daley's, right?'

'Daley?'

'Aren't you a Leaker? I am.'

'How do you know about Daley Jope?'

'Danny told me, so what?'

UltraViolet swallows. 'There'll be a huge fuss now you're gone.'

'That's why I'm not coming back.'

I'm not coming back! An echo of the Stevie on The Beak. How much has he grown up since then?

'Come on, then,' Vi says, a bit roughly. 'What are we waiting for?'

Two dots on the desert head for the Glade, creeping very slowly under the heat-haze. Just as slowly, a little distance away, a lonely figure extends its patrol into a dreamy loop after a dog.

The figure heads for the Glade. It has no helmet on.

'Jazzie?' it calls now and then.

A smaller dot just ahead of it heads at full speed towards the gloom of the trees, on a direct line of collision with the two figures headed from Thoreau. A sound just reached its keen ears – *arroo—roo—aloo!* The Rottweiler crosses the desert like a bullet shot from a gun.

'Sikes, come back!' Headingley stumbles, wakes at last as if from a dream, sees her dog disappearing .'Where are you going – SIKESIE!'

The small black dot moving at full speed converges on the two figures ahead of it nearing the Glade. A drumming sound on the ground takes shape into a blob in the heat-haze.

'What is that?' Stevie wonders.

The blob grows legs, a head – explodes into a large Rottweiler pounding along the desert floor with swags of flesh jarring under it.

'Oof! Sikes! No!'

Three dots on the desert meet, as Sikes cannons into Vi. She shifts huge paws from her chest to her shoulders. 'Yes. I love you, too.'

'How come he likes you so much?' Stevie hides behind her.

'Maybe I smell better than you.'

Maybe she has a point. Covered in hostile hospital smells, he could easily be mistaken for one of those patients routinely flushed out of the Glade.

'Down, Sikes! Good dog!'

'Can ... you ... hold ... him ... for ... me?' A strange figure ahead drops its hands from its mouth.

'Sure,' Vi bellows back.

The strange figure lurches towards them.

'Violet Niles! That you?' Bo Headingley walks with difficulty, veering right, correcting, veering right ...

'What is wrong with her?' Vi watches in disbelief.

'Looks like she took some sol.'

Headingley waves vaguely. 'Don't move! I'm coming!'

'Sometime this century.'

'We could run – she'll never catch us.'

'Sikes'd get us.'

'Not if we took him with us. You won't let her send me back, will you?'

'Don't worry, I've got her in my pocket.' I *see you flip out. Do something weird. I see you out on your own.* 'This one's on me,' Vi says.

At last they can see Headingley's expression. The lights are on, but there's no one at home. Nothing but an empty Adviser's shell, with all the lights blazing ADVICE.

'Saw you on telly this morning,' Stevie remembers.

Headingley blinks. 'Telly?'

'On *Sunspots*. So how come you're here?'

'Ever heard of a recorded interview?' Vi smiles for her. 'Bo.'

'We meet again, Violet Niles.' The Adviser looks badly sunburned. 'How are you doing?' she adds, after an interminably long moment.

Arrooo–roo–loo–

Headingley twitches. 'Wild dogs. They're everywhere.'

Suddenly Sikes takes off like someone lit a fire underneath him. Headingley watches him affectionately. 'Patrolling the Glade. Leakers there.'

'How about putting this on?' Prising it out of her hands, Vi puts Headingley's helmet on for her and snaps down its BluScreen visor. Headingley looks at her dumbly through the Blu.

'Don't you want to know what we're doing here?' Vi says.

'If you want to tell me.'

The Adviser seems paralysed. Vi plucks *The Little Book of Sun Manners*, a Solar Advisory Service Handbook, out of Headingley's top left-hand pocket. 'Sunstroke, here we are.' She traces the symptoms with her finger. 'Headache, nausea, raised temperature, confusion and collapse.' She looks at Headingley critically. 'You should get some help.'

Headingley scans the horizon. 'Got my dog in that Glade.'

Look at her skin, Stevie's glance says.

'That rash —'

'Photo-sensitive reaction.'

'Will it wear off?'

'I just need some shade.'

'Let's go,' Stevie says simply.

At first the weeds get more frequent. Then hardy grasses appear. Gradually starry mosses make the going softer underfoot, as the shade of the Glade reaches out. Out of the brain-deadening heat at last, the shadows make a new world. Insects and butterflies appear like jewels. The swish of prairie grass reaches them, a blue-green sea around the trees, the wind rifling through it in ever-changing patterns like waves.

Sikes waits for them joyfully, his tail flagging his path like a sail. *Swish-swash*, through the sea of grass. Woody smells of summer jump up like small explosions of taste and memory, as stems squish underfoot. The dark aisles between the trees ahead smell deliciously of pine. Even the shale underfoot, the remains of a quarry under the bluff, has a dank, stony fragrance all its own.

Suddenly stiffening, Sikes arrows off through the trees.

'Sikes! Wait!'

'What's with him?' Stevie wonders.

A series of crashes in the undergrowth. *Arroo — rah!* That howl again.

Headingley shrugs proudly. 'He smells a wild dog, he's gone.'

'Hope Reeve's all right,' Vi worries. 'I left her ages ago.'

Reeve's trying her left side, when the thunderbolt hits the trees.

Omigod, what is it?

Something black and bulky, charging out like a cannon, flinging froth as it comes! Hurling itself on poor, blind Blacks, the dog she just befriended, now a snarling ball of hate and fear, fighting for its life! Reeve jumps up in panic, a sharp pain in her ankle sending her flying forwards on to her hands. The thunderbolt, it's —

'Sikes! Get off! Go away!'

Furious snarling and flying froth. She can barely tell one dog from another.

'Where did you come from? Get *away!*' She doesn't know she's crying. Tears run down Reeve's cheeks. Her body shakes with shock as the savage sound of the dogfight rips through the peace of the Glade.

The spruces bend like aunts. *What* a fuss about nothing ...

Reeve crouches, trembling, the taste of blood in her mouth. The hideous snarling rises to a furious pitch as the dogfight travels over her bag, scattering the few items she has with her. She wants to beat Sikesie off. What can she do but avoid them, try to keep out of the way?

It seems like a fight to the death.

Blacks tries to follow Sikes's movements, sensing where the attack may come. Sikes circles like a cocked gun, watching for an opportunity to surprise him. Suddenly Sikes springs, bowls Blacks head over heels, goes for the throat. Blacks wriggles free, snapping hysterically. Sikes darts in on the rebound and savages his shoulder and neck. Blood glistens on Blacks's poor, patched hide. It's only a matter of time.

It seems so desperately unfair.

'Leave him alone, he can't *see!*' Reeve finds a stick in her hand. Sikesie has Blacks by the neck again. Blacks backs away, still held by Sikes. The fight moves over a tree-stump; around Reeve. Reeve hits bits of Sikes whenever she can see them. 'Get off him, go away!'

Trembling, the blood from her bitten lip somehow the

taste of the fight that totally absorbs her attention, Reeve misses the shouts in the trees.

'*Reeve!*' Vi appears under the spruces.

Doesn't matter how she got there. 'Help me get him off him – please!'

Headingley appears at a run. 'Sikes! Leave it! No!'

Collaring her dog, she snaps on his leash; drags him away, slavering and complaining, rolling his eyes to check her mood – did he do well or not?

'You took your time.' Reeve wants to be angry. Instead, she starts to cry.

Vi hands her a tissue. 'Took a lot longer than I thought.'

Stevie appears.

'They let him out?'

'No, I did.' Vi indicates the side of her mouth. Reeve finds the blood, cleans her lip.

'Where did that dog come from?'

'Blacks? He's blind. I think he's the howler in the tunnels, remember?'

How could anyone forget?

'What, he followed us here?'

'He's been around us – the Undercliff, that time –'

'Are you sure you're all right?'

'Look what Sikes did to him.' Reeve examines the sticky wounds in his side. Blacks obligingly licks her hand as he cleans them.

'Only skin-deep,' Headingley says. 'Nice dog. Too bad he's been out in the sun.'

Reeve considers the boiled-looking Headingley.

'You brought an Adviser, thanks for that.'

'Bo's all right,' Vi says.

Reeve nods to Stevie. Stevie says, 'All right?' back.

'Your van around here?' Vi quizzes Headingley.

'Under the bluff – not so far.'

'Think we can carry her to it?'

'Just let me lean on someone – I need to get out of this Glade.' Reeve collars Vi and Stevie. Together it's not so bad. Hop, lean, swing. Hop, lean, swing. At last blinding shafts of light widen between the trees.

'Reminds me of the Undercliff.' The swish of the pine-tops overhead reminds Vi of the swoosh of Stevie's heart-monitor, unhitched on an empty bed back at Mirabeau County Hospital. *Swish-swoosh*, like a heartbeat, a deep pulse of perfect calm, far from the hectic sun, the pines like the pillars of a cathedral, maybe the church of summer … so hard to emerge into full sol from this safe and sheltered place, to face the glare of day, things you might have done …

'Moisture levels fall every year,' Headingley distantly reminds them. 'These spruces are tough, but UV'll see 'em off. Only a matter of time.'

A battle, like Blacks and Sikes – inevitable, Reeve thinks.

'The Undercliff'll last,' Vi insists.

'Maybe.'

'Permanent shade,' Vi reminds them.

'Nothing's permanent.' Headingley comes to a halt at the edge of the Glade. Before them the desert swelters. 'I thought you'd have known that, of anyone.'

'Why's this dog blind?' Stevie means Blacks, obligingly trotting after them.

'Cataracts. Too much UV.'

Stevie slips on his sunglasses quickly.

'Dog probably belongs to a Leaker around here.'

'Are cataracts painful?' Reeve asks.

'Never had 'em, myself.'

Vi flips Headingley's visor down. 'Now you won't,' she says.

'Dog's been following you, huh?' Headingley narrows her eyes.

'We heard him howling near my house. That was – ages ago ...' Vi's voice trails away as waiting for them, throwing a wild shadow, they suddenly see a wild man – shades of her vision of Headingley alone in the desert, only this time the vision speaks. 'Hey!'

'Some half-baked tunnel-rat,' Headingley Advises. 'Let me handle this.'

'Does he need help?' Reeve wonders.

'Hey! Need any help?' The wild man walks towards them, loose-limbed arms swinging, the whites of very blue eyes settling on Reeve. 'Don't mind the way I look. Been on the run for a while. Hi to your Adviser, by the way.'

'Who is it?' Reeve stares.

Stevie shrugs. 'Dunno.'

The wild man stops at a polite distance. Under his matted hair, his face is streaked with dust. Young but filthy. Tame but wild. Extending a hand to Reeve, his teeth flash white as he smiles.

'Thanks for rescuing my dog. Name's Jope. Daley Jope. I think you know my brother?'

Chapter 11

Lions & Whistlers———

Daley Jope produces a lead. 'Here, Milt. Good boy.'

'How do we know he's yours?' Reeve challenges, as Blacks jumps all over him deliriously.

'Someone else wants a blind dog?' The wild man rakes his hands through his hair, puts on a civilized smile. 'Reeve, isn't it?'

'You're Danny's brother?'

'Right.'

'You're Daley? *The* Daley?' Stevie's eyes glisten.

'Didn't mean to freak you out. A layer of dust makes a good sunscreen, if you have to keep moving.'

Reeve says, 'You mean, you're —'

'Leader of the Leakers.' Headingley's hand falls heavily on his shoulder. 'It's my duty to Advise you, you may be in grave danger of exposure. Experts say that living outdoors can lead to terminal skin conditions among other —'

'Follow your own advice.' Daley shrugs her off. 'I normally have protection.'

The beginnings of dim recognition stir in Reeve's mind. 'I thought Daley Jope ran away.'

'Three years ago. With the dog. I renamed him Milton because of his eyes.'

'Milton – because he went blind?'

'No, because he writes poetry,' Daley deadpans, fondling Blacks, now Milt, his fingers discovering weals.

'He got in a fight,' Reeve says. 'But he gave as good as he got.'

'Always does,' says Daley. 'Been living rough, him and me, under full sol now and then. That's how he lost his sight. I tried to Protect him, but what can you do?'

'You must have a lot of rads,' Vi calculates.

'You're …?'

'Violet Niles.'

'Off the scale.' The wild man holds Vi's eyes. 'Like everyone else at Thoreau.'

'My ankle's the size of a melon,' Reeve says. 'Can we go now, please?'

The journey back continues in the Advisory Service trailer that Headingley left under the bluff. With Headingley at the wheel, Sikes, Vi and Daley upfront, Reeve in the back with Stevie and Milt, they start up in a replay of the strange run home from the Undercliff they experienced not long ago. But this time things are changed; not least of them, Bo Headingley.

'You OK to drive?'

Headingley ignores her.

'Strange twilight,' Vi says. 'Strange sky.'

Headingley drives expressionlessly. They reach the bullet-riddled sign. Beyond it, the highway dips. As they pass, the sky, glowing with whorls of pink light, shows them the pond at Thoreau.

'Funny sunset.'

'Yeah,' Headingley says at last.

'Thoreau Compound.'

'Yeah.'

Daley watches the crumbling mansion slide by.

'Want us to drop you off anywhere?' Vi asks.

'And you're going …?'

'Home.'

Daley shakes his head. 'Things to do in town.'

Headingley turns on the radio. Strange roars and whistles fill the cab.

'Get those lions and whistlers!' Daley whistles himself.

'What happened to the radio?' Vi stabs stations.

'Disrupted.'

'By lions?'

'Actually by a magnetic storm. Lion roars and whistler waves – natural radio emissions.'

The sound of the earth's electromagnetic field responding to a storm of magnetised particles ejected from the sun lets in an interrupted broadcast:

'… magnetic storms associated with solar eruptions may cause surges in power lines, causing flickering lights and black-outs, resulting in … *WHOOO–WHEE–WHERR–BIP–BIP–*'

'It's got a rhythm,' Vi says.

'*BIP–BIP–BURR–WHOO–WHEE–BIP–BIP–BURR* … other terrestrial effects of magnetic storms may include static interference and interrupted transmisson of radio, television and ... *OO–WHEE–BURR–*'

'News disappeared.'

'Interrupted transmission.'

'From flares?'

'Magnetic disturbance.'

The radio waves predicted their own interruption too well. Vi turns the radio off. You can have enough of those spooky, circular rhythms, like nothing's at home in the universe except some cosmic answering machine.

'Looks like those solar storms kicked in,' Daley broods.

'Upsets the Net,' Vi guesses.

'Upsets everything.'

'Affecting the ozone layer, right? Letting in more –'

'Ultraviolet. Exactly what we need.' Daley looks grim. 'At least it disrupts defence communications. Puts the Vale down, as well.'

Vi pictures lions and whistlers filling the databanks at the Vale, growling into the control room, dials and monitors overloading with the giant whisper of the magnetosphere.

'How about social security? I'm Hot,' Vi explains, 'and I wondered if there was a way –'

'You can get back into the system? Disruptions like this, you can do what you want. All you need is a new number. You can have one of mine, if you want.'

'Isn't yours Hot too?'

'See the compound there?' Daley turns as the plain allows them a long look back at Thoreau, disappearing in a blaze of flame as the entire sky explodes in fiery red. 'I'd say those freaks burned the place down, if I didn't know an auroral sky.'

'Looks like the world's on fire.'

'Excited aurora. Intense solar wind.'

'We nearly there yet?' Reeve calls.

'What do you know about Thoreau?' Vi probes.

Daley shrugs. 'I crash there. No tunnels, for starters.'

'Thought I saw some.'

'Old stuff. Disconnected. Places for rats to crash.'

No tunnels to town. Take a risk to get there. Take a risk to get out. Slip in and out of the system, in and out of doors. Inside and outside, a whole part of your life. Seems pretty normal, somehow.

The lights of Condorcet wink out as they approach them.

Reeve wriggles forward. 'What happened?'

'Surges in power lines. The radio. Where were you?'

'Look at that sunset.'

Daley grunts. 'The entire sky goes red like that, that's a magnetic storm.'

If only it *were* the sun going down, a pulse in Vi's head beats. Let it be the sun going down, or the sky's too big and too red to ever be normal again. *Seems like the sun, seems like the sun, like the sun going down to me* ...

'Either a storm or the world's end,' Vi finds she's said aloud.

Headingley brakes suddenly.

'Why are we stopping?' Vi wonders.

She hasn't said a word for a long time.

'You all right?' Vi says.

Headingley pulls on the handbrake and opens the door. Steps out into the middle of nowhere under a blazing sky.

'Wait, where are you going?'

'It has to do with the desert, that's what you said, isn't it?' Headingley turns and walks away, stumbling only once, the fiery sky winking off her badges as she disappears into the night.

It has to do with the desert. It's going to happen soon. That's what you said, wasn't it?

'What are you doing? Come back!' Vi calls after her. That blank expression. Wobbly walk. 'Why are we stopping here?'

'Not again.' Nick Niles opens the door with a candle in his hand. He squints past Vi into the darkness. 'Where's the Adviser?'

'She dropped us off.'

In fact the Adviser dropped herself off. Then Daley drove them home.

'She's got sunstroke. Pretty badly. I think she's losing her mind.'

Why didn't you stop her? Reeve had said.

How? Vi had insisted.

Headingley's expression had turned inward already as she drove out over the plain. When she saw the Nightjar in her headlights, she'd pulled on the handbrake and followed him into the darkness, his tracks leading her on, until the shouts from the trailer died in the silence, and the red desert night closed around her.

We should go after her.

Let's get Stevie home first.

She's got sunstroke; we should stop her.

Like to see you try.

The argument had raged on, while the figure grew smaller and smaller, the aurora flashing off its helmet. Sikes had slept through it all. And finally Daley drove them on, the headlights cutting a swathe through darkened Condorcet and flashing on the domed Niles garden.

At last Daley killed the lights. 'This is where I get out.'

'You don't have anywhere to go?'

'No.'

'Why not stay in the trailer?' Reeve had asked.

'Too much heat.'

'Where will you stay?'

'With me.'

They turned to look at her. 'Well,' Vi had said, 'Daley and Milt and Sikes – they can stay with us.'

'The Adviser lost her mind?' Nick searches the darkness and finds, instead of Headingley, a man dressed wholly in dirt. 'Who's this?'

Vi introduces him. 'Daley – my father, Nick Niles.'

'Mister Niles.'

'Nick.'

'Sikesie and Milt – I said they could stay a day or two.'

Nick raises his eyebrows. *A filthy man and two dogs?*

'We bumped into each other. Danny Jope's brother. Hope that's all right, Mister Niles.' Daley looks at him penetratingly.

'You'd better come in.' Nick frames the words with difficulty. So few come in at the door.

Daley looks huge and wild against the gleaming chrome surfaces of the studio. He looks around. Whistles. 'Isn't it Doctor Nick Niles, the ultraviolet guru? Or should I say Doctor BluShield?'

'Not a polite question, when you just stepped in at my door.' Nick smiles mildly. Vi knows that look in his eye.

Daley meets it. 'No offence.'

'None taken.'

'Dad, Daley's had a hard time.'

'Oh?'

'He lives out on Thoreau Compound – can't get back there tonight –'

A crash from the kitchen breaks the tension as Milt knocks over the single ewer of water they have in the house, with the solar-powered pumps temporarily down.

'How about a shower?' Nick suggests, before the wild man sits down.

'Difficult, with no water.'

'I'm sure you'll manage, an outsider like you.'

'Isn't there some spare capacity?' Vi looks from one to the other. What is happening here? 'I'll fix you up,' she says.

But still it seems a funny thing to do – to fix up a BluShield Solar Shower from the BluShield rain storage tank over her room to warm an outsider, very probably the chief campaigner against the company who made it, with its stored stream of sol-heated water ...

Chapter 12

Living with the Enemy

'Feeding the lambs will take place in five minutes ... anyone wanting to feed a lamb with a bottle, please make your way to the Barn for "In Touch With Animals" in five minutes' time ...'

The lambs have gathered already when Vi arrives in the Barn. Butting each other and rearing up with sharp little feet that set their metal gates ringing, they already smell the milk in the bottles that Meadow Farm staff are handing out to the children waiting to feed them.

What a tug! 'Hold it upright – that's right.' Staff correct Vi's movements with the bottle. The lamb sucks so greedily on the nipple, it's really quite hard to hold on! The lamb's wool is surprisingly thick and springy, its body seemingly frail but actually quite strong, something you'd never know unless you touched one. Someone hands her a tiny yellow and brown duckling. *Oh no!* No sooner is it in her hands, than it springs out and lands on the floor!

'Stronger than they look, aren't they?' the girl says, recapturing it. Vi only handled it for a moment, but at least she knows now how ducklings *feel*. Next she touches rabbits, piglets, goats, and actually gets to feed deer. The rabbits feel silky and soft, the piglets bristly. Cats chill on the wall. They go wherever they want, and she knows what cats feel like. 'In Touch With Animals' lets you feel and get to know animals you otherwise wouldn't.

'You can *say* that, and do what you do?' An angry voice cuts through the Barn.

'I do what I do because I have to.'

'But unthinkingly to play a part –'

'We all play a part.'

'To say, this is not me, this is just what I do for a job, surely that's irresponsible?'

The argument cuts through the Meadow Farm experience, no matter how hard Vi tries to shut it out.

'I contribute to international experiments.' Nick again. 'I don't need a rank outsider to come here and patronise me.'

'Our only responsibility is to make the right decisions.'

'I take responsibility *and* enjoy a good lifestyle.'

'Must be tough. I sympathize.'

'In a pig's eye, you do.'

The argument changes the texture of 'In Touch With Animals', ruining the illusion and fuzzing the goats.

'Argue downstairs, why don't you?' Vi rips off her headset and listens.

'Why not help alternative strategies? In what way is being the public face of BluShield OK?'

Switching to *QuestHolme* in disgust, Vi attempts to game on. Time for something more gripping – Edition Seven, maybe. *Graphics and personal involvement greatly enhanced*, says the guidebook. *Enter at your peril. Over thirty thousand solutions. The best a Quest can get.*

Vi goes into the bathroom and washes her face. She looks at herself in the mirror and the girl with the violet eyes looks wearily back at her. These arguments. They'd get to anyone. Even greedy little piglets would trample over one another less.

'In what way do you contribute?' The hardness in Nick's voice travels easily up the stairs. They've argued the last three days, ever since the power came on.

'By living outside bad systems?'

'Well, hold the front page.'

'Friction in the machine is all right to a point. But when friction *is* the machine, let there be no more machine ...'

'Meanwhile, you're eating my food.'

'I eat better in the tunnels.'

'Maybe you'd better go back there.'

'Maybe I will.'

UltraViolet splashes her face; looks up slowly in the mirror, water streaming like tears. 'Please can you stop?' she yells.

Downstairs in the kitchen, she opens the fridge and finds a frosted bowl of brown rice and three packs of dull grey butter. 'Better go shopping again.'

'Tell your friend. He ate most of it.'

'What?'

'Did he encourage you to go outside? Put us in this spot?'

'Dad . . .'

'Sleep all right?' Nick changes subject. Bangs the kettle on furiously.

'Can you *please* stop arguing?'

'I'll leave, now the power's back.' Suddenly Daley's framed in the door, more intensely blue-eyed than ever. His eyes take in Vi but not Nick, as though Nick has been somehow dismissed. 'If that's OK with you.'

'I'm upstairs doing blood work.' Nick jams toast in his mouth, swings up the stairs with his coffee.

Vi nods. Daley's eyes are on her.

'Whatever,' she says, meaning, *Why are you looking at me like that when you never even noticed me before?*

'Guess what?'

'Is that Bruce?'

'Stevie's home.'

Not Bruce, not now. Should've left it on answerphone.

'That's so brisk – he's all right?'

'Came home with Reeve the other night. She sprained her ankle, met him at the hospital, coincidence or what?'

'Coincidence – is that what your dad said?'

'They sent everybody home.'

'They did what?'

'Hospital records went down in the storm. Everything got mixed up. He came home in hospital PJ's, but he's cool.'

All that effort to smuggle him out, how ironic is that?

'Can I call you back? We're doing something quickly, then Daley's got to go.'

'Daley who?'

'Never mind – he's really all right?'

'He just ate two bowls of cereal. They let them out on the way back, he even stopped at the Glade for some fresh air. Can you believe they did that?'

Interesting editing of the truth. Even a solar storm comes to Stevenson Stallingham's aid. He doesn't even have to try. Talk about a lucky face.

'Um,' Vi says. 'Got to go.'

'Talk to you later.'

'Brisk.' Vi kills the call.

'Friend of yours?' Daley asks.

'Stevie's brother.'

'Hospital-boy has a brother?'

'Bruce, he's such a freak. What are you doing anyway?'

'Checking sleepers.' Daley keys commands into a bedroom terminal.

'Sleepers?'

'Messages posted during periods of solar disturbance. They wake up with the system.'

'But the system has woken up.'

'So now I have mail.'

'Why not use e-mail?'

'And have the Vale scan it? No, thanks.' Pocketing a Stored Power Attachment from a port in Vi's machine, he spins around in his chair. 'Ever heard of The Out?'

'Leakers go out all time.'

'I mean The Big Out.' Daley gives it capitals. 'Interested in joining us?'

'Not until I know what it is.'

'Mass march outside.'

'And the point is …?'

'To make a point.' Daley returns to the screen. 'So now we have the form up.' Tapping in a few details, he hacks easily into the countrywide Identity Bank, pasting in her photograph. 'Enter your new number here … and here …'

Vi watches the numbers wink up, one form validating another. 'So will it revive my account?'

'Not yours – Dolly Jope's.'

'What do you mean?'

'Has to be my initials, or it isn't system compliant. Sorry, but you're a Jope.'

'Couldn't you at least have put "Donna"?'

'I can keep the number, if a name's that important –'

'Dolly's good,' Vi says quickly.

'You should get new cards any day.' Daley files a request under 'Credit Card Applications' in the Bank. 'Far as they know, they're lost.' He shuts down. Logs off. 'Now I have to go.'

'Quick coffee?'

'Better not.' Daley rolls his eyes upstairs.

'He won't come down. Please.'

'Quick one then. Thanks.'

The kettle takes an age to boil. This is one visitor she doesn't want to leave – why? The tap drips coldly into the sink. *Stay*, it says with every drop. *Stay, you don't have to go.* Daley comes in before she's poured.

'You don't see your brother,' Vi comments, busying herself with the coffee.

'No.'

'Why not?'

Daley adds cold water, downs his coffee in one. 'Because the old man just about ran me out of the house.'

'I don't mind being your sister instead,' Vi says.

Daley flinches. 'Sister?'

'Dolly' Jope. 'Funny name to make up.'

Daley turns and shoulders his bag. 'See Danny much yourself?'

'I don't see anyone much.'

'What, you Quest instead?'

'I just did In Touch with Animals.'

'One of those new immersives?'

Vi nods. 'Add your own props.' She tweaks out a tray of feelies from under the bed. 'Fur and bone, sponge, leather, bits of fluff and wool – anything for texture. Horsehair for horses, wool for lambs, cotton-wool for a duckling. Calves' tongues are harder, but a wet flannel does it for me.'

'How sad,' Daley says simply. Vi slides the tray away. Sympathy's harder to take than never touching an animal again. How sad to sit in your room with a headset on and a bit of wool in your hand, imagining you're feeling a lamb.

'Hey,' Daley says. 'We all feel it.'

'And anyway, where do the mothers go?'

'What do you mean?'

'A theory of mine.' Vi wipes her eyes with the back of her hand. 'Notice they're not at home? That's because they're all in Afterminster, having tea and scones in some perfect tearoom somewhere with horse-brasses on the wall.'

'Afterminster?'

'Just another simulation. Like the whole rest of my life.'

'So use that anger to change things.'

'The way you do, you mean? Following people, that's changing things?'

'What do you mean?' Daley becomes very still.

'I know you were following us. The tunnels, the Glade. You were one step behind us all the time. That's why Milt was howling – you lost him on the way.'

'He wasn't lost. I left him. He howls because of his eyes.'

'You haven't answered my question. Why were you following us?'

'OK, I didn't know he was your father. Reeve was my connection. I thought Reeve knew where he was –'

'Nick, you mean?'

'I thought I could persuade him to help us, but that was always a long shot. But we knew he had a daughter. I kind of remembered you actually –'

'*That's* why you helped me just now?'

'There are things we need to know about BluScreen.' Daley's eyes are like hard blue chips. 'Why is it so expensive? People could have gardens if one big company wasn't sitting on the technology. We need inside information.'

'Why didn't you come out and ask me?'

'I'm asking you now. Only you can do it. Will you help us open the doors?'

The sound of Dr BluShield crossing and re-crossing the room above her puts a shiver down UltraVi's back. The computer screen blinks. *Access Granted*, runs the message across all systems. *Dolly L. Jope. Social Security number 38985.*

Will you? Daley's eyes say. *Will you help us open the doors?*

'First, I don't know if I can. Second, I don't know if I want to. Smiley says work from inside.'

'Smiley?'

'Sells the *Sol* on the Boulevards? Now he's a Solar Adviser.'

'Davis Nailey. I know him. Stay away from that man.'

'Working from inside to improve things, that's what my dad's doing, right? So sometime the price of BluScreen comes down —'

'Suppose someone cornered clean air. Put the sun in a bottle.'

'I wish.'

'We need to reclaim outside. BluScreen's for everyone, right?'

The computer screen blinks. *Access all systems granted. Please option Open or Quit.*

'What kind of inside information?' Vi asks at last.

'Warehouse locations, formulations for UV-Selectives, delivery movements, production costs, materials, etc. We need all this to access the operation.'

'You mean — blow the whistle on my father?'

Daley watches her closely. 'That's exactly what I mean.'

'You'd better go.' Vi gets up. Shepherds him out. 'Go and see your brother, I'll be in touch.'

Daley turns at the tunnel-mouth. He looks at Vi. 'Do I have to?'

'Family closeness, open doors — deal?'

'You mean it?'

'Go and see your brother.' Vi lifts the tunnel-flap. 'Tell him I'll see him sometime.'

Later Nick comes up. 'Vi? You there?'

'Where else would I be? Direct to Net, site: Violet Life, all Pisceans this week ...'

'What are you doing?'

'Horrors, what does it sound like?'

'Daley left.'

'I know.'

'Mind if I join you in a little escape from reality?' Nick sits down beside her. 'What have you got? Quest Seven?'

'What's up?'

His face looks strained. 'Reality's too hard sometimes.'

Vi tips him a headset. 'Over twenty thousand solutions. Choose the way to go.'

Choose: be close to your family, or betray them for someone you like a lot over something you're in a unique position to help with. Betrayal or approval? Inside the family, or outside the knowledge that the way you're living is wrong?

It's a minefield out there. Thirty-six total levels. Over thirty thousand ways to finish a scenario.

Enter at your peril.

Chapter 13

Shopping Dad:———
Part One

Betraying your father's a funny thing. It never gets any easier. Just when you think you've got it covered, he looks up over the breakfast you brought him, smiles, says, 'Thanks a lot,' and the guilt begins all over again.

The girl with the violet eyes goes into the bathroom and washes her face, looks at herself in the mirror, pops out her violet contacts, sees a lot more clearly now.

Daley had said a few things before he left. Get anything to me, watch for the Face. How will I get anything to you? Vi had asked. I'll send a messenger. Daley had winked. Be in touch.

Sikes appears at the door and yawns.

'All right,' Vi says. 'I'm coming.'

Incredible how much Bo's dog eats. He ate up all the cereal already. Now it's ancient steak-and-kidney pies from cans shaped like frisbees that someone scored from Wesley many moons ago. 'Miss Milt, don't you?' Vi puts the tin on the floor and Sikes noses it around the kitchen. Might as well eat if you're bored. What else is there to do? Milt hadn't wanted to go, you could see that at the time. But Daley had said, 'Milt.' And the old blind dog had hopped after him.

Missing Milt. Missing Daley. Time for breakfast. This morning it's hash browns and eggs. Potatoes from the sack in the pantry, a couple of eggs for a treat. Grate the potatoes. Squeeze out the fluid. A dab of oil in the pan, throw in the grated potato, press down, brown for a couple of minutes, then break in a couple of eggs. Chicory coffee, toast – and breakfast is served.

Vi watches herself in the microwave oven door. Nice going. Why are you doing this?

'Knock, knock.'

'Who's there?'

'Breakfast.'

'That time already?' Nick feels for the clock as Vi nudges open the door with her tray of eggs and guilt.

'Aren't you presenting a paper today?'

Nick groans. 'Abby at nine.'

'Abby who works at the University?'

'Taking me to the conference in one of those buggies. These Uni runabouts make a change from walking. Abby applied for one next week.'

'So how come she has one now?'

'Staff car for general use.'

'What do they look like?'

'Golf buggies. Solar powered. Could be handy for you and me.'

'You work for the University sometimes. Can't you apply for one anyway?'

'One per household.'

'So?'

'We thought she might move in.'

Vi sets down the tray. 'What do you mean, move in?'

'Abby and I, we've been seeing each other a while now ...'

'You didn't tell me.'

'No.'

The eggs look up at both of them. 'They might be over-cooked,' Vi says, simmering inside. *Nick Niles here. Sorry I dropped a bomb on you. I would discuss it with you, make you feel a part of this family, if I weren't such a freak —*

'How would you feel about that?'

Vi shrugs. 'I hardly know her.'

'That's the point. You'll like her.' Nick sits up and rubs his hands. 'Hash browns, my favourite.'

Vi leaves him to it. 'Enjoy.'

'Vi —' he calls her back.

'What?'

'Perfect eggs. Thanks a lot.' He winks in that stupid way people do when they know you're not really placated.

It's nothing, Dad. Nice timing with the announcement that your girlfriend moves in next week. It helps me make up my mind. I had booze instead of a dad, then I had a microscope. Now I don't need you anyway, if I ever had you at all.

'Vi!'

'What?'

'Ten-past nine, I'm late.' Nick clatters downstairs, turns at the bottom, bounds upstairs again. 'Vi! Where are you! I lost my notes!'

The sound of books hitting the floor.

Vi joins him coolly. 'These?' Rescuing a sheaf of lecture notes from the printer, Vi flips to the introduction. '"Dirty Babies, Clean Bill of Health" – nice title.'

'Gimme.'

Instead of handing them over, Vi begins to read. 'We have developed lifestyles in which our homes are ultra-clean, where children who are well-off play on computers rather than getting into rough and tumble in the mud outdoors, where they get cuts and bruises and get used to fighting off infection …'

'Vi. Please.'

'… but with the new UV-Selective plastics, year-round access to soil microbes can be a reality.' Vi looks up. 'At a price.'

'That's enough. Hand them over.'

Nick snatches his notes. Vi follows him downstairs.

'So how do we play in the dirt, when BluScreening your garden costs a fortune?'

'I don't have time to discuss it now.'

'BluScreen's for everyone.' Vi hangs over the stair-rail. 'It's only a matter of time before the technology gets out.'

'Not if we get our way with Patents.'

'No doubts about it, then.'

'You think I bought this house with doubts?' He's

shrugging on his coat, angry now. 'Of course I have doubts. I take the money and swallow them. Do you think that makes me feel good?'

Vi rescues a stray page of notes from the stairs, scoots down to hand it over. 'Didn't mean to upset you before you went out.'

'You won't tell your mother you went outside, if she calls?'

'Not unless you do.'

'Attagirl.'

'Dad —'

'Feed the dog. Eat what you can find and be cool.'

UltraVi watches him go, the movement in the tunnel tracing his departure wending towards a rendezvous with Abby at Locke Junction, and a lift to the BluShield-sponsored Immuno-Suppressive Disorders Conference, which will be video-linked to every concerned institution under the sun.

Some kind of lecturer. Some kind of dad. Some kind of Doctor BluShield.

Outside the studio window the sun beats down on the garden, probing the strength of the BluScreen and gradually undoing its polymers. Beneath it, lettuces simmer but are able to grow. At five-thousand NetCredits a metre, it costs about as much as silk. Looks a lot like it too, the halo of heat above it throwing out all the colours of the rainbow ...

Sikes rests his head dolefully on UltraViolet's knee. We're living a lie, Sikes, she thinks. All this — by denying BluScreen — a garden — to everyone who can't afford one. Where is she, Sikes? The image of Bo Headingley rises before her. How could she, Violet Niles, have allowed someone crazed with sunstroke to walk off into the desert to die a lingering death by sol?

Vi flips through a magazine, though she hardly ever reads these days; but still Bo Headingley looks out of it with every article, no matter how remotely connected, to do with sunshine or sickness. '*Vit. D Deficiency Made Me Go Blind, Claims Vegan.*' She should visit Sammie's Sun Parlour herself, have a D-Activator Programme.

When was the last time she went? Down on the Boulevard Smiley would wait to sell her a *Sol* when she left, lightly tanned from the D-Activator, a Graduated Programme of UV Exposure administered under Strict Safety Guidelines ...

Instead of ringing Sammie's Sun Parlour for an appointment, Vi boots up the computer, tries a few of Nick's passwords, then probes some sly little draft files to do with his job.

A BluShield order form flickers up. Some other BluShield stuff. Daley wanted locations. No address for headquarters. Vi digs deeper, accessing secure files with inspired guesswork based on personal knowledge of Nick Niles's mind and circumstances. It's when you're alone that betraying your father kicks in. When you've nothing to lose but his company, which you're about to lose anyway. Still no address. This is silly.

Bee-de-beep.

Violet stabs Quikdial, speaks to her wrist. 'Mum?'

'Vi – what are you up to?' Grace Evans's voice sounds tired.

'Nothing much, except –' *Except that we went outside. Dad didn't even try to stop us, the second time.* 'Except that we've got a dog.'

'But Nick hates dogs.'

'He's a Rottie named Sikes. We're minding him for a friend.'

Oh, and we might be accused of stealing an SAS vehicle? Reeve rolled it down the road. I think it's behind her house, but it's only a matter of time ...

'Ten weeks till Solstice Day.'

'I could come over earlier.'

'Of course, but we'll be away.'

'You and Patrick, you mean.'

'When winter comes, you'll be here for three months. We'll have picnics, a hamper, the lot.'

Vi eyes the BluShield order form lighting up her screen. *Five hundred metres? Five thousand? Please click on your requirement.* 'So when you order stuff over the Net, how do you find out where it comes from?'

'Addresses, you mean?'

'I have to click on "requirements".'

'How do you send stuff back?'

'They collect Returns.'

'Commercial Listings?'

'Not listed.'

'Give me five seconds. I like a challenge. What kind of company is it?'

'Plastics,' Vi says cautiously.

'OK, I've got listings on disk.'

This is too specific. Daren't mention BluShield. Why would she be ordering any anyway?

'I actually need stuff on manufacturing processes and storage. It's just a college project, never mind.'

'Never mind – you sure?'

Nothing like using your mother's job in television research to betray your father, occasional consultant for every channel but hers. Daley wants more than this anyway. No one opened any doors by sitting on the fence.

'Got to go, someone's coming.'

'Everything OK?'

'Fine.'

'Call me.'

'Soon. I promise.'

But not too soon. You don't call me. It hurts.

Buh-boom-boom, buh-boom –

The vibrations of someone blustering up the tunnel can only mean that tunnel-smell that greets Vi on entering the kitchen. At the same time, the tunnel-flap lifts over …

'Smiley!'

He straightens his hat grimly. 'Violet Niles, I am Advising you now –'

'Remember when you used to smile?' Vi interrupts him.

'It's my duty to Advise you, stay in until further Advice –'

'We stay in too much, don't you think? I told Daley Jope he should go and see his brother –'

'Daley Jope is *here*?'

'He left the other morning,' Vi says a little uncomfortably.

'Jope is Notifiable. Where is he now?'

'Gone. I don't know. In the tunnels.'

'To put up more of these.' Smiley unsheaths a roll of dog-eared posters from his rucksack. 'Takes me all morning to remove these. "A New Community on Hume Island." All signed "Random Squires".'

'So Random Squires postered the tunnels.'

'Random Squires is a myth.'

'What, you think it's Daley?'

'What do you think?' Smiley watches her.

'I think,' Vi says, 'you've changed.'

Smiley rolls his posters, slots them into his bag. 'They found the vehicle from your last little outing, you know.'

'Headingley walked off. She disappeared.'

'Leaving you with her dog, her home, her belongings.'

'Actually, yes. She's Sun Struck. She didn't report in or anything?'

'Not since one thirty-eight, the afternoon of the ninth.' Smiley extends a clipboard. 'Sign here ... and here ...'

Vi scans the form. 'Permission to be Monitored?'

'That's a twenty-four-seven.'

The electronic Tag that will signal Vi's whereabouts to Central Advice, twenty-four hours a day, seven days a week, closes over her wrist.

'Do I have to wear this?'

'It's Advisable.'

'Meaning, you'll monitor me anyway.'

'Outside Against Advice sets no conditions.' Smiley tucks away his pen. 'Let me ask you for that doctor's coat.'

'But you gave us the suits to go out in —'

'The coat. And any passes.'

Vi hammers upstairs and fishes in a cupboard; hammers down again.

'It's in this bag.'

'Be cool.'

'That's it? You're going to go?'

'Things to do, people to Advise. I make Full Adviser, my first month — star report, two Leakers.' He winks. 'Keep your sunny side up.' He ducks into the tunnel. Has a second thought. 'By the way, those Solar Suits. You find bits of them everywhere.'

'You mean —'

'Overdates. Polymers fused. No Protection at all. Advisory Service dog. Coming with me, right?'

He makes a move to grab Sikes's collar.

Sikes rumbles, then explodes. Smiley dives into the tunnel. Sikes punches through after him. The black rubber lips of the tunnel-mouth smack together after them.

Vi puts her head through and shouts at them, the sound of Sikes barking at Smiley's departing form in the rattling, green-lit tunnel completely drowning her out. 'Were you spying on me all the time, even when you sold the *Sol*? What about working from the inside? WHAT HAPPENED TO THE TROJAN HORSE?'

Chapter 14

Supergrass

```
GraceEvans@Apollo.com
Vi's welcome here from 1 March till Solly,
if you and Patrick have plans. I can pick
her up when I have time, or maybe we can
arrange to meet. She wants to take up a
martial art, so I fixed up Self Defence.
There's an insurance form to fill in.
Grace, are you OK with this? — Nick.
```

She's welcome here, *if you and Patrick have plans*. I can pick her up *when I have time*. That's what you get when you spy on your dad – things that you didn't know, you didn't want to know.

UltraViolet opens more e-mail. Show me no more surprises, no more tiny betrayals. Things like being exposed to many more rads than you thought you had, thanks to Smiley and his overdates suits (why would he *do* that, anyway?) are actually easier to deal with than these casual little giveaways. Less painful, and more relevant, is the good stuff on BluShield Worldwide:

AlanMugler@Blu.com

Re: That darn documentary!

Al,

I think we should refuse to comment.
Protesters are going to read more into what
we deny, than if we don't say anything.
Don't know if you spoke to Alison, but my
advice is to zip it. Of course the
documentary was damaging, but products
arriving at Bayle can change schedule to
avoid trouble. Those Leakers are guessing
anyway. Call me later.

Nick.

Products arriving at Bayle. Seems a television documentary put
the cat among the pigeons at BluShield, so Nick had had to
sort it out.

Three conclusions from this latest information are:
a) BluShield have a depot at Bayle, b) Near Vi's mother's
house, how convenient is this?, c) Protesters maybe know
this already, so d) More information is required, perhaps e)
A map of the depot?

Vi goes to Consultancy Files; options 'BluShield', then
'Locations', then 'Bayle Base', then 'End Product Storage'.

Bingo! A detailed map of the depot flickers up, showing
a complex range of buildings. When 'Point of Sale' is
optioned, the screen co-ordinates cross over a large

warehouse, the kind of warehouse, surely, that Daley's Leakers would like to find in their Solstice Day Lucky Stocking.

Vi zooms in. The warehouse is the largest there. Conveniently sited near the boundary fence, it has to be filled with cool spools of BluScreen, ready to roll out and green the desert, if gardeners everywhere could afford it. If only she could throw open the doors. Roll up with a lorry-load of Screening, dish it out to everyone, like the Mother Teresa of Plastics – Here, Screen your garden – go grow lettuces, tomatoes, squash, french beans, broccoli, chives!

Big corporations like BluShield have cashed in way too long. How to let Daley know the layout of local headquarters? The *Sol*, for one, would love to know about the BluScreen mountain.

Rolf! Rolf! Rolf!

Furious barking from the kitchen. Sikesie sounding the alarm. Maybe Smiley came back. Or Nick.

Rolf! Rolf! Funny, doesn't sound like Sikes.

The sound of breakables shattering downstairs; claws capering over floor tiles; something else falling over. Vi reaches the kitchen in time to save the coffee pot, as the tail of a blind black dog sweeps it off the worksurface.

'Milt! What are you doing here?'

Wildly mixed up with Sikes already, Milton greets Vi enthusiastically. 'Back already? Daley lose you? No – maybe he didn't.' So many things going on. No accident this dog returned. *How will I get anything to you? I'll send a messenger.*

Milt puts his paws on her chest.

'Daley send you? What?'

I'll send a messenger.

A tiny pellet under the dog's skin rolls between her fingers. Slipping into the workshop, Vi returns with a scanner. Passing it over the dog's rump, she finds that her hunch pays off.

'Thought so! A microchip!'

The tiny message decodes as: 'Reach Me This Way'.

But how?

Imprint the chip with information, then replace it. So simple, so unlikely she'll be able to do it. Nick might know. Behind Milt's collar — a syringe. Suddenly she sees that she might.

Vi makes the call: 'Dad —'

'What's wrong? I'm about to speak.'

'How do you write a message to a microchip?'

'At a microchip plant.'

'But if you can't?'

Moments before addressing a conference, anyone else might have asked her to call him back, but Nick's prepared to think a little. 'I guess you might try "Inscribe". Write from Inscribe to the chip. That's if you have a chip.'

'You need an attachment, right?'

'I'm on — speak to you later.'

Now using Dad to betray himself, Vi kicks it up a notch. Almost there. Think it through. I have a microchip. I have a program to write to it with. I have map coordinates for the warehouse where rolls of BluScreen lie hidden. *I have the means to send information to Daley undetectable by the Vale or by* anyone else unfamiliar with a certain dog's behaviour. All I need is a port attachment. Maybe the office drawers – yes!

Vi pops the pellet from under Milt's skin with her nail. 'Only tiny – won't hurt.'

Loading the attachment with it, she pops it into a port on her computer. Carefully optioning 'Write to chip' in the Inscribe program, Vi hits ETCH when the map is on-screen, electronically etching information across to the microchip. Removing the attachment from the computer, she takes out the tiny pellet. Finally she searches the kitchen for a gross can of 'Mister Brane's Faggots'.

Lucky Milt can't see the syringe.

'Here, then. Lovely offal.'

Shutting Sikes out of the room, she puts down the bowl of food. As Milt wolfs it, she puts the syringe to his rump. Squeezing down the plunger, she injects the pellet down the thick-ended needle, inserting it just under the skin.

'All done.' Vi rubs the place. 'No worse than the vet's ID under your shoulderblade, is it?' The other, numbered, pellet has been in place for years. Talk about a sleeper.

This is one message that will only sleep until Daley scans it up, wherever he is. Vi pictures his face when he sees the map of the Bayle Facility – how big is that storage warehouse? No way will his jaw not drop when he sees the BluScreen mountain they may have suspected, inside it. Maybe he'll tip off the *Sol*. Organize a tunnel protest. Now that the information's out there, people should be able to use it.

So tiring, this spreading the word.

The girl with the brown eyes goes into the bathroom and washes her face yet again. An anxiety behaviour always with her, it shows her things in the mirror, sometimes only her eyes with no coloured contacts ...

Suddenly the mirror clears. Bo Headingley staggers through the desert. Scabby buzzards circle above her. The sun beats down. A house looms in some trees. Headingley makes for it – falls.

Milt nudges Vi's knee.

The desert in every direction. Vi tries to towel it away, but a terrific sadness wells up. Milton watches her blindly. The needle-prick is one more in a collection of mystifying events that brought him a meal today. Of course, it's Daley he wants.

'Come on, then. Time to go.'

Attaching the syringe to his collar, Vi posts the blind dog through the tunnel-mouth with enough information, in the right hands, to blow the UV-Selectives market wide open.

'Daley – Go!'

He doesn't need much persuading.

As soon as Vi releases him, the Howler in the Tunnels pads away. She nips to the window to see the tunnel rock as he passes. Go, Milt, with your loaded skin. Then she watches television with a new sense of satisfaction.

Shopping Dad has its upside, after all, in the shape of a new sense of mission. In the shape of a scruffy black dog with cloudy eyes, already as far as Locke Junction.

BluScreen's for everyone, right?

Vi sees him padding along; pictures the network of

tunnels, the final bolt across open ground to Thoreau, if that's where Daley is. Good old Milt. Sense the way, don't go wrong. Molecules left by Daley's shoes hitting incredibly sensitive odour detectors in Milton's nose, biological sensors to match anything the Vale can dream up, will guide him on his way more surely than eyes.

Go, Milt, with your loaded skin.

A message in a bottom.

Enough information, in fact, to blow open all the doors ...

Chapter 15
The Face ————————————————

Talk about an inside story. Events are unfolding without UltraViolet having to leave her room. Her bedroom begins to feel like a nerve-centre. Is the action at Thoreau this brisk? Or is Leaker Central vague and hippy-fied, defending everyone's right to wander around in dungarees and earrings shaped like parrots? Maybe Thoreau freaks browse the desert, collecting brushwood and 'signs'. Maybe Headingley's one of them now. Or maybe she lay down and crisped.

The vision of Headingley rises up yet again, always with a glance in the mirror. The idea that *the warning she gave her made it all come true* never leaves UltraViolet for more than a moment. You let her walk away. Do something. Help her. By doing what she Advised me against? Going outside again?

The knot of guilt and inaction grows tighter inside her chest.

Vi hasn't been out of her room in three days, when Danny Jope, of the rubber neck, calls her out of the blue. Reeve calls just before him, when a single and Monitored word is spoken: 'Trouble.'

'Reeve?'

'They found the trailer.'

'Yeah. I know.'

Then Jope, Danny Jope, his voice unusually cheerful: 'I saw my brother.'

'Your brother?'

'My brother, Daley – he ran out, remember?'

'He came to visit you?' *He kept his side of the deal.*

'I saw him on the Boulevard. I shouted, but he walked on.' *He didn't keep his side of the deal – yet.*

'Maybe it was someone like him.' People listening. Zip it.

'He's here, I know he is. I know he's going to contact me soon –'

'He ran out years ago. He could be anywhere.'

'– probably any day now.'

'Talk to you later. I'm Questing, all right?'

Vi kills the call. This game of cat-and-mouse. Feels like she's been playing it for ever. Headingley extends a sun-baked hand in the full-length bedroom mirror. Will you help us throw open the doors? Will you? You abandoned me. Do this to make up. Will you? Will you? Will you?

Vi turns the mirror to the wall. Escaping into *QuestHolme*, she buries Headingley in DesertQuest 3 as the most like, and therefore unlikely, place to find her.

A ripple moves along the tunnel outside, pushing radon gas in front of it into the house. The tunnel-mouth smacks in the kitchen.

So what? Nick coming in.

A news broadcast overrides Game Function as the walls

detect his presence. First there's a Public Access television interruption, quite familiar by now. This series of rants from different freaks calling themselves The Face has bypassed Vi so far.

Until now. Now a wall-high face fills the room.

The Face of Stevenson Stallingham.

'Hi, Sunseekers.' It's a strange message. 'This week's holiday destination is a hotspot near you. Bail out of those indoor blues. More information, Monday.' He smiles again. 'Remember to pack those last-minute items.' Winking, this time: 'Keep your sunny side up. This is The Face, signing off.'

Wall Functions default back to gameplay, plunging the darkened room into the Seventh Edition of QuestHolme. Henchmen crowd around her. But Vi's pulse races before she fires a shot.

Keep your sunny side up. A strange echo of Smiley's favourite saying, still they broadcast the information so quickly! This week's destination. A hotspot near you. Bail out of those indoor blues. More information Monday.

Something big must be brewing. Probably a coded reference to a protest at Bayle on Monday. Stevie the Face – helping too – where did he broadcast from? A Henchman brings down an axe on her head. Vi parries. Chops him down with the edge of her hand. Dodges and moves on, firing. Stevie's wall-high face, Headingley, Jope, Reeve – all annoyances and wonderings are soon buried in the violent headrush of the Quest.

*

Two hours later, and Vi burns through to the Japanese cycle of *QuestSeven: Forbidden City*.

Ahead of her stretches a hall of armoured figures. One of them holds the key to all following levels. One of them holds an assassin – which?

The oriental armour has been made to be light but flexible. Strange wicker breast-plates wink with jade hinges. Curling, lobed helmets are designed to turn away a blade-edge. Curving swords gleam in every gloved hand in the Hall of Armour.

Violet Niles creeps past the armoured figures in search of a QuestKey.

Nick puts his head around the door. 'I'm going out with Abby – want to come?'

'Where is there to go to?' Vi checks her Tag is under her sleeve.

'The Minster Mall?'

Ahead of Violet Niles, a pair of eyes gleams under a helmet. On either side the armour is empty, the oriental swords pointing downwards. Vi creeps along the row. Slowly, one sword rises.

'No, thanks.'

The lights of the game play on Nick's body. He's a lump in a tenth dynasty warrior's side. 'Been immersive lately?'

'Headset's weird.'

'I'll fix it.'

The sword falls but Vi leaps over it – turns and nails the assassin. She walks on into a room filled with hexagonal boxes, one of them holding a QuestKey. The Guardian stirs, a dragon this time. She can dice with him or fight him for it.

'So, we'll see you later.' Nick lingers at the door.

'Get me some Power Mix, will you?'

'With what?'

'Try this.' Vi hands him a card.

'Dolly Jope?' Nick scans the card. 'What, we're illegal now?'

'They put us outside the system.'

'And what "they" would that be?'

Vi eyes him coldly. 'I'm surprised you don't get one of those big-shots you know to pull some strings for us.'

'You think I haven't tried? Long term, there's no problem, short term −' Nick taps the card on his nails −'I need blood products, gauze, vitamins − but Dolly Jope ...'

'It's just a name. Daley fixed it for me.'

'You like Daley.'

'Yes.'

'I like to get arrested through someone my daughter likes.'

Vi plays on.

'I said, I −'

'Dad, can you go now, please?'

Nick retires, all spotted with dragons. The Guardian falls on Vi, sending her back to the Hall of Armour and robbing her of three vital Keys.

'Mind the dragons.'

'Power Mix.'

'If they have some, it's yours.'

Finally the doctor departs. The battle for QuestKeys rolls on, until at last Vi droops on her cushions, her infrared glove sensors sending crazy signals to the walls, her sleeping brain empty at last but for dreams, while the Quest locks into a holding pattern, endlessly repeating its Overture over her sleeping body ...

Some time later Vi wakes up in Drogo's Castle.

Count Drogo looms over her: 'Headset. Here.'

Vi sits up. 'Was I asleep?'

'Just drooling.'

She takes the headset. 'Thanks.'

'Can't see anything wrong with it.' Count Drogo turns out to be Nick, weirdly lit by the loop advertising *Transylvanian Quest*. He hands her a tray with a flourish. 'You left these feelies downstairs.'

Vi takes the tray of objects. The tray of props looks as pathetic as usual – crucifix, bible, garlic, peeled grapes for eyeballs, canned spaghetti for guts, all the usual stuff for Gothic Quest. The stained-glass windows in Drogo's Hall, alias UltraViolet's room, give Nick a blood-red backlight. Drogo's teeth flash. 'Your frogs are dying in the bath.'

'My frogs?'

'Remember them? Did you look at them in three days, or what?'

'Doing it next, all right?'

'Meanwhile.' Nick shells a couple of cards from his pocket. '*QuestHolme Futures*, Edition Eight – enhanced graphics, supposed to be unbelievable.'

'You just got me this?'

'I think our friend Dolly Jope did. Enter the number on the card, download anytime you want.'

'Edition Eight?'

'Just out. Plus Power Mix for the trip.' He throws down packets on her bed; watches as Edition Eight graphics begin to flicker up. 'Thanks for bringing me the stuff, Dad,' he finishes sardonically.

'Thanks for bringing me the stuff, Dad.'

'No problem.' Nick lingers again. *I feel a little guilty over Abby, so I got you something you like.*

'Can you go now? I'm tired.'

'Yes, of course I can.'

The bars of a striking new overture fill the room as Nick quietly closes the door, the hot new edition of *QuestHolme* travelling instantly down the wires.

'Bye, Dad,' somebody calls, switching to immersive, looking sightlessly after him in their headset ...

UltraVi washes her face, drops in new coloured contacts, then bags up the Power Mix for a long-distance journey outside. Hi-energy food in a resealable pouch. Remove all bits of the devil's food, dried banana. Whose idea was that anyway?

The packing is simple and speedy; nothing but survival rations, plus the ugly Blu-suit she welded together in the workshop the day Jope and Roddy came round, it seems so long ago now. Seams of the suit are still pretty tight. Now to test them out.

There's something else. It doesn't take more than a minute or two in the most sensitive of Nick's Video Conference Files.

Search By Name or Position? the personnel menu enquires. Position? *Chief Executive*.

Company? *BluShield Worldwide*. Trigger word? *Confidential*. A minute or two sees it done. Send to Net? *Yes, Please*. Close? *OK*. It's complete. She's been busy just over three minutes ...

Her frogs, she feeds last of all with captive flies from a trap by the tunnel-flap.

Looks like they might need releasing soon. Can't keep 'em long after their arms appear. Arms mean developed lungs, gulps of air, live food. It's then that they need live insects to eat, or you find them dried up like raisins.

'Be free soon or die,' UltraVi whispers above them, the only god in their sky. Be free to hunt for yourselves, wherever live insects can be found ...

But this isn't about insects or frogs, or places they're free to meet. This is about Bo Headingley. About doing something real for once, getting up and going out and saving a person from dying.

UltraViolet straightens herself in the mirror. Sees a warrior there, for sure.

She picks up a lead. 'Sikes. Come on.'

And she plunges out of the house with only a bag and a dog, the slap of the tunnel-mouth behind her the final goodbye to the back of her father's head, as he sits watching Network Seven, on which a newsflash suddenly breaks.

'And breaking news just in – a security leak at Blu-Shield –'

'Vi!' Nick bawls. 'Come quickly! Take a look at this!'

Doctor Nick Niles's head is as tall as the building.

What did she expect?

Vi's heart jumps as she sees her father's expression on the video wall. Over the heads of a gathering crowd, Nick Niles, ultraviolet consultant to BluShield, discusses the public face of BluShield with its Chief Executive in a private interview covering the entire side of the Minster Mall.

Private, that is, until his daughter posted it over the Net. Pounced on by newshawks in minutes, flashed around video walls at most major food co-ops, already the word in the tunnels is that BluShield have sat on BluScreen like a major dog in a manger.

Seeing Nick incriminate himself is different from hitting a few keys. UltraViolet, what did you expect when you sent secret stuff to the Net? Such big news, so soon!

'So you're saying we say nothing?' Head honcho Tom Fairbanks puts his fingertips together.

'The technology's cheap. Of course we could provide BluScreen for everyone,' Nick Niles confirms. 'We're not a charity. That isn't our point. We build our market slowly.'

'You saw the documentary, I take it?'

'We have no obligation to make this technology available.'

'Can you spin it so that we look as if we don't rule this option out?'

'We have every right to protect ourselves.'

'We don't need to look like we're keeping people in.'

'It's our fault the sun got hotter?'

Dad! Don't say any more! Nick's mouth opens and closes, raining down damning words on an ugly crowd. *Dear Abby, move in as soon as you can. Escape with Dad in that little Uni runabout you applied for. Drive like the wind over the desert in your stupid little buggy, to take him far away and make a new life. He can't live here any more.*

UltraViolet turns away. Family ties, all that stuff, that's all behind her now. All that remains is Headingley, guilt, and the quest to do something real. The hot breath of the tunnels blasts hair in UltraVi's face. Sikes drops into step behind her. One place to try first, that mansion with trees around it she 'saw' Headingley fail to reach in the mirror three days ago. Makes a match with a crumbling old place under a bloody red auroral sky. Thoreau Place, if anywhere, has to be worth a try.

Behind her the giant faces dig themselves in deeper with every word, till a buzz of indignation rises from the crowd and rides on the wind in the tunnels.

Run, UltraViolet! No turning back!

Dr Niles's private files. Smuggled out by his daughter. Broadcast on every smart surface in sight, plus all sides of major tunnels. Nick Niles, opening his mouth and blowing off his career with secrets his daughter let out, the daughter he made blueberry ice cream for and tucked in so tenderly that time when she fell asleep in the Quest …

UltraViolet runs on through the tunnels, heart in her mouth, Sikes at her side, her father's giant mouth spelling betrayal at every major junction. Still he has nothing on Vi.

Shopping Dad to every thankless tunnel-rat, to help people you never met live outside, at the cost of everything *inside* your home and your heart. Let's hear it for the Queen of Rats. Now that –

– that's *real* betrayal.

Chapter 16

Travels with Harty-—Noakes

Popping out of a tunnel by night, Vi removes the Tag from her wrist and snaps it around Sikes's neck.

The adjustable band fits him easily. Wait till he starts doubling back and bounding around. The screens at Central Advice should look like pinball machines. Pity the dot they'll be monitoring will be their own Advisory Service dog, and not, in fact, Violet Eveline Niles, alias 'Dolly Jope', alias a prime Leaker once more, now leaving Condorcet limits. That is, once they part company, her and the Adviser's dog.

For the moment they're a team. Violet Niles considers the desert ahead. Somewhere out there – Headingley.

'Go, Sikes! Find her!'

A whiff of Headingly's jacket salvaged from the trailer, that cold night Bo left the trailer and walked out into the night, gives Sikesie the right idea.

'Smell her out, Sikesie – where is she?'

Sikes sniffs the desert wind. He stiffens; wags his tail. His nose points unwaveringly east.

'That way? Is she? Really?'

Sikes's tail beats against the tunnel-mouth, the last tunnel-mouth before the security fence between them and open desert. They had to be under the Vale for their rescue mission. Maybe not the smartest exit position, but the one nearest Leaker Central at the strange and crumbling mansion known as Thoreau. Vi eyes the searchlights above, while Sikesie strains to go. 'Wait for the light to come round ...'

The searchlight sweeps its bright white eye over the backs of the gleaming tunnels that make up the warren of Condorcet, now shining coldly between the moon and the lights of the Vale which outline colossal listening dishes monitoring a million conversations.

Somewhere beyond the dishes, Thoreau sleeps in the hills, or maybe hatches plans all night to keep one step ahead of the system. UltraViolet can practically feel the outrageous freedom of planning to *come and go*. The crackle of a fire as they burn their Tags, fry their Factor 82, toast the wild wind outdoors; the sting of dirt and hunger, freedom and judicious sunburn; their right to decide for themselves. A million images sprout in Vi's sensation-starved brain. This way you can go mad. Thinking too much makes of your own teeming mind the monster that you have to live with.

The searchlight sweeps past them – Go!

Vi releases him. Sikes leaps. Hurdling the fence, he's gone in a single motion, the drum of his pads in the darkness her only guide into the desert ...

One direction, one dog. One purpose under the moon.

As the sun rises over a pond some two hours later, her guess is proved right. UltraViolet 'saw' Thoreau in the mirror. Thoreau is where Headingley's trail leads Sikes. All trails meet as one.

It definitely looks better from a distance. Behind its impressive frontage, the back of the house looks shabby. Vi descends on the pond from a westerly direction, details clearing as she goes. A garden Protected by a BluScreen dome turns out to be a small vegetable patch tended by someone grubbing around under a patched-together wigwam of Blu. Someone she feels she knows, from the fuzzy outline visible through its crooked seams.

Sikesie lopes down the slope towards the crumbling old house, once pretty statuesque. He throws himself at the patchwork dome and the hidden gardener inside it. Inside the house, a face appears at the large ground floor bow-window. Sikes goes mad when he sees it, barking and jumping up.

'Sikes! Shut up! I'm coming!'

Easy for a dog like Sikes to take a walk on the wild side. Not so easy for someone with only the vaguest idea what they're walking into. *Aroof! Roof! Roof!* Someone has to shut him up. It's only six in the morning. Gathering all her Ki in her chest, UltraViolet follows.

Inside the crumbling old mansion, the rising sun shafts in over a glass case sheltering a collection of tiny golden bowls. Each bowl is slightly more golden than the one in line before it. 'Tenth Dynasty Lacquering Techniques' a yellowing label tells no one.

Sir Merton Harty-Noakes, who collected the bowls in 1836, looks down from his portrait over the sleeping bodies dotting the carpet of his old home. No one cares about the lacquering process now, or the wicker-armoured warriors by the door. Even the canoe made with the intestines of an elephant-seal fails to raise an eyebrow; on their way to the pantry for a bowl of dried beans or flour no one notices it, anyhow. No use for explorers now. Having plundered the world to bring home his collection, Harty-Noakes fails to wow.

Who would have guessed the worthlessness of gold and silver compared with their weight in BluScreen? Foreseen that the stately home of an explorer would be one day inhabited by freaks?

Only UltraViolet, now closing rapidly on the house. Those oriental turrets don't go at all with the style of the rest of the place — why do those Tenth Dynasty warriors from the Hall of Armour in the Japanese cycle keep playing on her mind?

Bo Headingley turns over in her sleeping bag under Harty-Noakes's disapproving frown. Through the open door, the plink of the fountain in the hall coolly enters the room. Here fish the colour of orange peel swim in a shallow pool.

The pictures lining the hall show the Harty-Noakes's travels.

Sir Merton and Lady Enola at the Marriage of the

Maharajah of Jaipur. Sir Merton and Lady Enola on camels; crossing the Khyber Pass; viewing Victoria Falls. On horseback in the Himalaya; the rosy city of Petra; giving their hearts to the silence of the desert in burning Wadi Rum. In Greece for Etruscan vases, which had been all the rage. Collecting the treasures of the wide world, completely worthless now.

Now Harty-Noakes's hats and trousers are used as gardening clothes. Someone cut off the tops of Lady Enola's tiny, narrow walking boots to make sandals for their six-year-old sister. No one values old things, except where they can adapt them.

The hush of early morning lies heavily in the empty corridors, until a dog begins to bark outside. The sleepers turn on the hard floor, but not a single one would leave. Tunnel-rats have been known to stay weeks, studying Harty-Noakes's papers, learning about a world wider than the span of a grubby tunnel, or three months' winter sunshine. Someone calling himself 'Random Squires' even circulated extracts from Harty-Noakes's Journal, to show the determination needed to explore not only a mountain range, but also part of yourself. Serialized for a time in Big Sol, no one read it much. The telly gives you the world, after all. No need to move a muscle.

A skinny black cat enters the hall and settles down to watch the fish in the pool. The cool plink of the fountain enters the drawing room; some sleepers swim in their dreams. Across the hall in the Study, a shaft of early morning sunshine lights up a case of daggers. The key to their cabinet lies under Daley's pillow. His sleeping bag rests beside them. But Daley isn't here, now. Daley went out last night.

Bo Headingley sits up suddenly. Barking. Where's the dog?

Hey, Susie. Sukey. Sikesie – that's it. Funny how people keep animals and have to get up to feed them. Funny why people do anything. What's the use in getting out of bed? Doesn't help sunburn get better. Moving makes it worse, but sleeping's impossible anyway. May as well lie around and chat, get up to speed on the latest with any freak who comes by. Lot of talk lately about Hume Island. A new community, etc. Sounds understated so far, but when they talk about restocking with goats and cropping the fields, the way they did years ago, in fact reclaiming the island, it can get pretty intense.

Rolf! Rolf! Rolf! Roof-roof!

Dog's outside. Headingley passes her hand over her eyes. Gets up and yawns at the window. Who is that out in the greenhouse, this time in the morning?

First time she felt like getting up in a long time. Days spent unconscious following her rescue from the desert haven't improved her any. Big dog outside the window. Looks like a dog she once knew. Stallingham working the garden. Who's that coming towards him like a train? Looks a lot like that girl – Headingley searches her memory, returning slowly but surely in the cool shade of Harty-Noakes's house – that girl with the funny eyes, Scarlet Piles? Darlene Styles? That's it – *Violet Niles*.

The figure draws nearer determinedly – *has* to notice the

fences soon, though Daley tore most of them down — emerges from the shade of the trees into full sol, keeps going ... and going ...

Headingley's all attention as the girl, more than a little familiar by now, marches across the garden dressed in bits of BluScreen, looking pretty unstoppable now.

Stallingham sees her. Drops his hoe. She marches up to the greenhouse, a crazy patchwork of BluScreen, frail and gaping in places. Still she doesn't stop.

What, she doesn't see the door?

Headingley watches with astonishment as without pausing or breaking stride, the girl calling herself Violet Niles bursts through the side of the greenhouse and rips her way on through ...

'What did you do that for?'

Stevenson Stallingham's jaw drops as a girl bursts into the greenhouse, fighting her way through the plastic like the Terminator or something.

'BluScreen's for everyone, right?'

A dog tears through after her. Jumps out again and barks at the house. A single frilly-edged tooth of Blu falls down slowly after her, opening a hole in the plastic.

'Some kind of code, is it?' Stallingham swallows.

'You should know.' Violet Niles looks searchingly at Stevie, last seen on television passing on coded messages, putting himself on the line as the friendly Face of Leakers everywhere. 'So how come you've got this dome?'

'We haven't, now you bust it.'

'I'm looking for Headingley.'

'If you mean that sun cop, she stays in bed moaning all day.'

'She's in the house? You rescued her?'

'Know how long this dome took to make?' Stallingham ignores her. 'How many people stole bits for it and sewed them together?'

'I haven't got time for doors.'

'You shouldn't have burst in like that,' Stevie blazes back at her. He hasn't changed since the hospital, except that he ran out permanently and his father had to accept it. Another Leaking Teeny. Happens all the time.

'Stevie. Look at my face.'

Stevie looks. 'Violet Niles.'

'Nice to see you too.'

Stallingham's face opens as he stops panicking and recognizes her. Has she changed so much? Bits of the BluSuit she made cling around her body, her hair's wild, but so what? 'What's going to happen at Bayle?'

'The Face, you mean?'

'You put out some information.'

'Location of stored BluScreen. Final piece of the puzzle.'

'You made the broadcast quickly.'

Stevie grins. 'Davis is hot.'

'Davis Nailey helped you?' *That would be Smiley.* 'I thought he made other people Hot. You know he's an Adviser?'

'Was.'

'Is.' Vi considers. 'Does he come here?'

'Sometimes.'

'You know he works from inside?'

'Inside what?'

'People's trust, if they let him.'

'He left anyway,' Stevie says.

'I sent the information to Daley, not Smiley.'

'In a dog's butt? Brisk.'

It *had* been a brisk way to send it. 'Where is he now?'

'Daley?'

'The dog.'

'Went with the Out party.'

'Where?'

'A holiday destination, where do you think?'

Milt's with Daley. Headingley's safe. Vi relaxes a little. None of the stuff at home is her fault. None of the stuff here is her fault, except for the hole in the wigwam, an excuse for a Protective dome, which is pretty pathetic anyway. Still, the vegetables look good.

'So how much UV does BluScreen let in?'

'Enough.' Stevie shrugs. 'Daley says it changes to block out harmful wavelengths.'

'Did you just plant these?'

Stevie nods. The elf of rhubarb grew green fingers overnight. From not being interested in gardening at all, he's out at seven a.m. to water in baby cabbages, each fainting now in its dark splodge of wet soil. Potatoes take up most of the dome, most of them labelled neatly 'Pentland Dell'. The light coming in, dimmed by seams in the plastic, feels nicely light and harmless.

'Can you keep off the carrots? I'm supposed to be thinning 'em out.'

Vi moves off them. 'So why are you gardening anyway?'

'Strengthen my immune system by contact with dirt, Daley says.'

'I thought you had drugs for that.'

'Daley threw them away.'

'So Monday, something's planned?'

'Tomorrow, over at Bayle.'

'You said Monday on telly.'

'Anyone who watches The Face knows it's two days before.'

'Would Davis Nailey know that?'

The frilly lips of the hole Vi made in the greenhouse grate together a little in a breeze that runs through the lettuces like a chilly reminder that anyone can betray anyone, at any time at all.

Stevie wipes his hands. 'Want to come in the house?'

'I'm on my way to Bayle.'

'Now?'

'How about you?'

'Later today.'

'Will Headingley –'

'She'll be there.'

UltraVi pictures Bo Headingley putting up her SAS boots on a marble table somewhere inside the house, strangely like a cross between an Italian mansion and a Scottish castle, close up. That watching face at the window, as she came down over the garden. Sikes made a bee-line for it. It doesn't matter now, but could it have been Headingley herself?

'Come to Bayle.' Vi eyes Stevie steadily.

'Later.'

'Now.'

'OK.' Suddenly parking his hoe, he makes up his mind. Light, flexible, Thoreau-like, he ducks through the hole in the greenhouse and waits on the other side. 'Come on.' Taking control again. How annoying is that?

Vi ducks through it after him. Tears a V-shaped frill off the hole.

'Don't!' Stevie says, though it's done now.

Violet drapes it round him like a cloak. 'Don't worry, when they drop the price, you'll have as much Blu as you like.'

'Maybe,' Stevie says, dubiously.

Maybe. Maybe not. But something's happening at Bayle. Stevenson Stallingham knows what, though he's a little tight-lipped about it. Taking the lead, he looks back. 'We'll stop at that first big rock. Got some water on you?' So young, so middle-aged, planning refreshment breaks already, his strange frilly cloak over his ears. 'I bet they'll be surprised when they see how much thinning I've done.'

And how the greenhouse is ripped from top to bottom. Vi pulls up her hood. Putting down her head, she follows in Stevenson Stallingham's footsteps. It seems like the easiest option.

When Violet Eveline Niles finally looks back at Thoreau,

the bay window stands wide. Someone pink behind it leans out. Embraces and lifts in a dog …

A black Rottweiler wearing an electronic Tag, which is funny when you think that Central Advice will at last be tracking Headingley, for whom they've been combing the tunnels of Condorcet for the last three weeks, at least.

Chapter 17
Outside Looking In——

Another night journey seems certain.

Most of the day is taken up in a long march to Bayle with detours between pools of shade, to avoid being Advised and Cautioned by Bayle Solar Advisory Service. Temperatures climb to the forties.

'See that industrial area?' Vi points out the towers of what could be a plastics plant in the haze.

Stevie rubs his eyes.

'Feel bad?'

'Ozone.'

'Let's go.'

Stinging eyes and a headache mean low-level ozone, at last easing off as the sun goes down over the classier parts of Bayle. This side of town is glossy, expensive, be-treed.

At nightfall they reach a Mister Kidney's, a scuzzy chain restaurant selling recycled animal products at the farthest end of the tunnel stretching east to town. The only good thing about Mister Kidney's is the view it gives over Bayle before plunging into the tunnel complex. Here the compounds are glossy, the area thick with domestic tunnels.

The outskirts of Bayle are where Grace lives. That would be UltraVi's mum.

'Let's eat,' Stevie says.

'At Mum's house.'

'Your mother lives around here?'

Actually she lives in Afterminster, where a cosy blaze always lights up the hearth, and Patrick doesn't exist. 'Why not?'

'Big houses,' Stevie says.

'Looks like BluShield's on the other side of town.'

'I'm hungry,' Stevie says.

'Daley and the rest of them are probably in position already for the protest.'

'Whatever,' Stevie says.

'Better get on – tunnels or overland?'

'Tunnels.'

The tunnels are clean and fragrant, better maintained by a mile, than the dismal burrows around Condorcet. Except that it would have been too close to his ex-wife, Dr Nick Niles would have considered buying a place in Bayle himself; he actually had the estate agents' details, until Vi had put her foot down. *We're not moving there. But why not? I hate it over at Bayle. What's wrong with Bayle? Too close to Mum and Patrick. Patrick's OK, he – Please can you drop it, Dad? There's no way I'm living in Bayle.*

Now here we are. In Bayle. Vi runs her hand along the tunnel wall, cool from the air-conditioning. Milton had padded through tunnels like these with Daley; had delivered his message carefully, igniting a whole chain of events. What must it be like to pad along here and not *see*?

'Poor Milt,' she remembers.

'Daley said, with a small laser op he could see.' Stevie turns a corner on to a junction between D'Alembert and Diderot Boulevards.

'Remove the cataracts, you mean?'

'*Big Sol!*' Shades of Smiley! 'Get your *Sol* here! *Sol! Big Sol!*' Hailed by a pretty prosperous-looking tunnel-vendor, *don't even bother,* Vi thinks, though the headline reads 'New Hume Community Needs Volunteers.'

Even the tunnel-rats are glossy in Bayle. He could have tried a little harder. He didn't even say 'Hi'. Beyond the junction, the smell of pine hits them strongly.

'Fragranced tunnel air.'

'Brisk.'

A sign informs them that residents have voted *Pine Breeze* ahead of *Alpine Meadow* as Most Appropriate Seasonal Aroma. Stevie and Vi thread a rattling side-tunnel, finally emerging at the Evans Compound.

'Unreal.' Stevie whistles, the change in the tunnel from black plastic to a transparent 'designer' domestic tunnel showing them a porch blazing with flowers around an expensively Protected front door. Nasturtium, Morning Glory, geranium and fleshy amaryllis – blooms Vi remembers surprising her afresh every summer, until Mum had got herself a boyfriend and summers had run into autumns of postponed visits, and finally to winters of Making Up For It.

A side door exits the porch to a baked-looking drive. The split-level house looks like an aquarium cut down the middle, displaying the fish inside it with the expensive interior lighting glowing through its Treated glass walls. Two fish in there now.

Grace Evans and partner Patrick. Vi realizes she doesn't know what his last name is. But there he is. Smugly visible dining with Mum, tastefully back-lit and probably dressed in designer black, expensive rimless glasses precisely placed on his nose. Grace will be in a kimono or something ...

'Are we going in or what?'

Patrick something-or-other. Who cares what Patrick's last name is?

Re-entering the porch, the Stargazer Lilies scenting the step send out such a strong fragrance that Vi has to stoop to examine them. Pink speckled throats and waxy petals. Saffron-yellow pollen. That knockout pong.

'What are you waiting for?'

Vi raises her hand to the bell. Already the house knows she's there.

'Go on.'

'In a minute.' She abruptly exits the porch. Stevie finds her in the bushes, where the floodlit garden meets the edge of darkness. 'We're not going in?'

'Not yet.'

Here the sweep of what would have been a lawn has been baked as hard as concrete. The glass walls of the house throw down a golden glow, glancing off pebbles and a single blue-backed beetle making a night journey over the drive. The dining room glows like a treasure chest with something precious inside it. Candles flicker on the table between them. Mum and Patrick, how cosy.

UltraViolet hugs her knees. The feeling of being outside, a watcher, sorry for herself, isn't entirely unpleasant, so long as the figures inside don't know that she's there. What did she think this would feel like?

Grace flickers by in a kimono.

'Your mum, right?'

Vi nods. The glamorous woman inside the house doesn't feel like her mother.

'Will she be surprised?'

Will she?

A man in black crosses the room with two plates of food.

'All right,' Stevie crows. 'Let's eat!'

Mirrored in the golden glow of the walls UltraViolet 'sees' a plate of dust. She looks again. It's rice, with a few hard peas. Her mother's face is old. Her hands make a ball of rice. The rice falls to pieces, writhes away as worms. 'I don't feel like eating now.'

'Shouldn't waste food if it's offered,' Stevie parrots.

'That's what your dad says, is it?'

'He says I take things for granted.'

'We never have regular meals.'

'So what?'

'At least your dad's a regular dad.'

'No such thing,' Stevie says with feeling.

The glossy meal goes on inside. Vi explores the feeling of being excluded, even luxuriates in it. This is what it's like to be *outside looking in* on a cosy lifestyle you can never be a part

185

of, your life or death nothing to the people inside enjoying their food and the comforts of a 'well-appointed' home. This is what it's like to be a tunnel-rat, permanently excluded from beautiful, warm and comforting things that other people take for granted.

Stevie follows the movement from fork to mouth. 'They've got spaghetti.'

'So deal with it.'

A pause.

'Why don't we go in?'

'Because.'

'I thought we were going to go in and eat.'

'I changed my mind, all right?' Vi stabs Quikdial and waits for Nick to pick up, watches Patrick top up the wine over the dinner inside, imagining the glug of the bottle as the wine curls into the glasses ...

'Anderville?'

'Dad.'

'Vi.'

'I thought you'd like to know, I'm at Mum's house.'

'Grace call?'

'I had to get away.'

'New 'scope's got a cracked lens.'

'Problems?'

'Nothing another three hours in the workshop won't fix.'

Nick's in another world, her mother would always remind her. You can share it, but you can't change it.

'I'm tired of it, Dad. I need to get out.'

'Out?'

'It's not so bad, but it lacks structure.'

'What does?'

'The house. Our life. Mealtimes.'

Patrick collects the plates. Grace throws back her head and laughs. Grace's dog, Ben, races back and forth behind the window, barking at the figures he can clearly pick out in the bushes. Grace squints outside, drags Benny away. Any moment now they'll drop the blinds.

'We're about to have dinner. Parmesan cheese.' Vi shows Stevie her wrist phone. Stevie clinks stuff together, makes eating noises. 'Spaghetti, wine –' Stevie shakes the water bottle –'candles …'

'I hate to rain on your parade, but you're probably eating overdates supermarket cheddar. They boil it up, compress it – bingo! Parmesan.'

'Thanks for that.'

'Grace there?'

Yes, and no. Grace flickers to and fro; enters the living room with a bowl of fruit. Patrick takes an apple. *Remember bananas?* he's probably saying. You have to be over thirty to remember bananas, so difficult to grow under Blu. Patrick's over thirty. Vi's met him maybe twice.

'I can't live with you, Dad. You're going against everything I believe in.'

'Isn't that a little extreme?'

'You're sitting on BluScreen.'

'That again.'

'Why can't you come out against them?'

'Maybe I did.'

'What do you mean?'

'That leaked interview – did you see it?'

'Yes.'

'Well, I might not survive it.'

Grace waltzes slowly with Patrick – how unbelievably corny. What will they be dancing to? Some classical theme morphed through airy electronics. How utterly grim they look.

'You used to have lots of ideas,' Vi says. 'Things that would change the world.'

'Guess I grew up.'

'Like everyone else with ideas? The people you grew up with?'

'Cancer stats, most of 'em.'

No wonder those left want the good life. Vi feels a chill through her bones.

'I have to go, it's dessert.'

'Let's talk tomorrow, OK?' Nick signs off, probably absorbed in the cracked-microscope-lens nightmare.

Vi switches Functions to Net for the night's star-chart. She checks with the star-studded sky. Orion wheels over their heads. Time for the moon in Pluto. Should warn those Pisceans a dilemma's on the cards. Accessing Voice Recognition, she begins: 'Direct to Net, site: Violet Life, all Pisceans this week …'

Stallingham dozes beside her, tired of being hungry, overtaken by the long day's journey.

A cold moon beams down on those left outside tonight, and on all the cooling landscape around Bayle. On animals forced to hunt by night and invade people's houses by day. On the tunnels of Bayle and Condorcet, where tunnel-rats bed down under newspapers and *Sol's*, or whatever else they can find. On Thoreau, where Sikes sleeps across Headingley's feet and the fire throws giant shadows over the wall, as those about to depart for Bayle toast marshmallows before they go.

Outside under the same moon, the chickens have escaped again. Attracted by a large hole in the side of the greenhouse, they strut in one by one. Gales of laughter from the house drown out the dry, pecking sounds of their beaks, as they eat their way through the lettuces. In the hall, the fountain plinks. The goldfish weave together while over them, a black cat waits …

Headingley rises. 'Come on.' And accompanied only by Sikes, she walks out under the moon. Everyone leaves when they want to. No one tries to stop her. No one ever stops anyone, at Thoreau. No one understands her at all.

On the hill above BluShield Headquarters, Milton sleeps under the same moon, until Daley says, 'Time to go.' Beneath them the warehouse waits, just a part of the giant complex turning out BluScreen by night under sulphurous chimneys.

'What a stink,' someone says.

'Plastics factory, what d'you expect?' A figure comes up the hill.

Daley rises to meet it. 'Ready?'

'Anytime you are.' Their ace in the hole, Smiley smiles.

No one sleeps outside Grace Evans's place.

Let's talk tomorrow, OK?

The Horrors end as suddenly as they started. 'Watch you don't leave yourself in an exposed position when you can do so much better this week. End "All Aquarians This Week", leave Violet Life, Exit Net and shut down.'

Stevie hugs himself. 'Something wrong?'

Nothing another three hours in the workshop won't fix. I hate to rain on your parade. Isn't that a little extreme? Let's talk tomorrow, OK? Nick's such a brisk parent in so many ways. Just not in the ways that count right now, because now, if never before, you have to be *inside* or *out*.

'I'm starving.'

'Isn't there anything to eat?' Stevie moans.

'Yeah, I brought a whole picnic – sandwiches, cake, pies ...'

Vi shares out the Power Mix and they disconsolately eat. Afterwards, Stevie calls Bruce. They actually talk about carrots.

At the same time as Vi Niles and Stevie Stallingham crouch at the darkened fringes of a garden bordering Bayle, inside the BluShield Facility on the other side of town Smiley is talking his way into Warehouse Three on the strength of a Full Adviser's uniform and a nice line in fake regulations:

'Routine inspection of sun-protection facilities for workers, yes?'

'At night?' the watchman wonders.

'Night is the point, my man. Don't let me keep you from your *Sol*.'

The watchman folds it away, embarrassed. 'Any Unit?'

'Start with Three.'

'You'll need Passes for internal gates.'

'Soon as you like. Bring it on.'

Once in possession of the right colour passes for that night, why would Smiley kill the sensors on a whole section of security fence and slyly release the warehouse doors to let in a bunch of Leakers? Leakers so ragged and sun-blasted, the rads off their clothing alone will probably fire the alarms? Why would he work against BluShield, when he just made Full Adviser?

The teeth of Davis Nailey gleam whiter than white in the moonlight. One by one, the Leakers filter in. The 'inspection' over, and the doors of the warehouse rolled into place once more, Daley takes stock. 'Awesome!'

On either side, giant rolls of gleaming BluScreen dwindle away into the depths of End Product Storage Facility Three, rows without end from ceiling to floor, as far as the eye can reach.

'Scary how much they have stockpiled.' Daley nails Smiley with the hard blue chips of his gaze.

Smiley rolls out his sleeping bag. 'Intense,' he has to agree. The Leakers bed down under more BluScreen than they could have imagined in their wildest dreams of Blu heaven; a Blu mountain, keeping the price of vegetables conveniently high for some.

Daley props his head on his arm. 'We have to trust you on this.'

'Goes double for me.'

'Your job, you mean?'

Smiley smiles. 'I'm thinking of getting out.'

'Heard you're giving out solar suits.'

'You hear some funny things.'

'Name Violet Niles mean anything to you?'

Smiley shrugs; smiles.

'She told me,' Daley persists. 'Sending people out in defective suits ...'

'Stop them going out again.'

'You mean –'.

'Suits are fine. Just covering myself.' Smiley pushes back his sleeve to expose an electronic Tag. 'On Probation myself. Monitored twenty-four-seven. What are you going to do?' His teeth flash wickedly in the darkness. 'Report some Leakers. Limited damage. Get myself promotion. Then I can be some use.'

Long after Smiley's eyes finally close in sleep, Daley watches him. He encouraged Vi and Reeve to go out somehow, while Monitored himself – then reported them for extra cred, then told them the suits were defective to keep them from doing it again? Nice try, but no cigars. Davis Nailey, charming but sly. Should have called you Tricky.

Sometimes you have to play both sides.

He's a puzzle, is Smiley.

Just which side is he on?

And Doctor UV – whose side is *he* on?

Still smarting from a conversation with his broker over falling shares in BluShield Worldwide, Nick Niles scans his

Consultancy files and detects a recent visitor. 'Cookies everywhere.'

'Hum?'

'Someone left their mark in the system.'

'Not guilty.'

Nick spins in his chair to face a woman with dark hair and eyes. 'Abby – do I disappoint you?'

'I'm thirty-six. Nothing disappoints me.'

'How about my relationship with Vi?'

Abby smiles. She's really quite nice. 'You're a recovering alcoholic. I'm glad you're alive. Nothing you do disappoints me.'

'Am I a hypocrite?'

'Is this about that interview that got out?'

'Vi wants solutions. I work for the problem. See, I could make a difference, but I don't.'

'Join the fair-weather club,' Abby says. 'We go in whenever there's trouble.'

'It's not fair.' Abby's son, Rawley, appears. A shock of dark hair frames his pale indoor face. 'I want to run Cohorts or Ravendale, but Violet won't take the headset off.'

Nick raises his eyebrows. 'Use the other one.'

'She's got priority gameplay.'

'Edition Eight has a guest-room, if she's Questing. Go in and fight her for it.'

'It's like she's fighting someone already.'

'Practising self-defence?'

'With the headset on? You should see her.' Rawley's eyes widen. 'You should.'

'You should see yourself,' Stevie says. 'You should get some sleep.'

Vi checks herself in the side of her mother's glass house. The choker with the bits of Blu-suit looks pretty wild. Spiky, back-lit hair. Great that she got sunburned down one side of her face and not the other. The effect is actually quite weird, with the burnished-looking eyes.

'Your eyes look weird.'

'Gold contacts.'

Stevie watches her check them. Once Ben the dog got put to bed, the house drew them like a magnet. Now just under the stilts supporting the golden box of the living room, discovery seems a real possibility. Especially with Vi looking in.

'Shouldn't we knock or go in?' Stevie worries.

'Maybe.' Vi checks her lips.

Stevie watches her, unsure what's going on. 'I don't know anything about you.'

'You're twelve, why would you?'

'We're neighbours.'

'No such thing,' Vi throws back at him. 'Neighbours is the name of some hoary old soap, that's all.' UltraViolet, facing her reflection in the mirror of her mother's house. Seeing through its walls the golden girl reflected there going inside. Chatting with her mother. Hugging her. Going to bed, warm, close, included. 'I could tell Mum.'

'What about?'

'BluShield tomorrow.'

'No way.'

'My mother works in television. She can get us some brisk publicity.'

'Daley said, don't tell anyone.'

'Until the day we tell *everyone* — that's the point.'

Stevie considers. 'How?'

'Mum works for Network Seven. They'll kill to get this first.' Vi rips a page from her organizer, dashes off a note.

'I don't know,' Stevie sulks. 'You should ask me before you do things.'

'Since when did someone die and you become king?'

'BluShield. Saturday. The biggest scoop of your life.'

Vi folds the note. It may lie unnoticed till morning. Grace may not even get up in time to get out to BluShield and do anything. Wake up and smell the coffee, Mum. Your comfortable life is a lie, like mine. You can put your head in the sand, but you can't live for long that way. UltraViolet slips the note under the door. Patrick laughs inside. The sound of crockery clattering. They must be washing-up together.

'What's wrong?' Stevie says. 'You all right?'

Vi sinks against the door. She feels exhausted deep inside her bones, crushed as a blind, white thing at the bottom of the ocean under millions of tonnes of pressure, feeling with its dumb, blind foot for something real to cling on to.

'I feel like I'm collecting clues, and none of them add up.' A bubble of self-pity bursts in her throat. 'I thought I was going to rescue someone. I thought it was going to be real.'

The feeling of being a small child sitting on the step

floods back, the time she hid with a loaf of bread and tore out the soft, pappy centre because it smelled so good, and every mouthful was naughty. The door smells of home and certainty, walks and trips to the beach, warm cucumber sandwiches, a cosy towel, baths with plastic toys in, all the old-fashioned things that burned away like stubble from a field, leaving dark, gritty, grown-up reality.

'Rescue yourself.'

'What do you mean?'

'You're strong,' Stevie says. 'You can do it.'

The door opens suddenly. A man in black looks down over the tops of his glasses at a girl wrapped in bits of plastic, and a boy in frightful denim dungarees that look as though they belong on someone else.

'To what do we owe this honour?' Under his foot a note peeps out. It's obvious he hasn't seen it. 'Violet and ...?'

'Stevenson.'

Patrick smiles sardonically. He should get out more.

'Well, well – Stevenson. I suppose you'd better come in.'

Chapter 18

Shopping Dad: ———
Part Two

Grace appears with a tray of smoothies. 'Stevenson?'

'Stevie.' He takes one.

'Violet.'

'Vi.' UltraViolet accepts the other, in exactly the same way, like a stranger.

'Your father know you're here?' Patrick turns down the music.

'I called him.'

'And?'

Not your place to ask. UltraViolet sees a boy hiding with a book on the roof of a shed, over-clever, lonely. Patrick looks over his glasses with that same faintly superior air now. 'He wants to talk tomorrow.'

'I see.'

'Would you like to tell us what this is about?' A vein in Patrick's head ticks.

No, you're not my father. UltraViolet considers the table, still littered with dinner things.

'You must be hungry,' Grace says.

'Stevie likes spaghetti,' Vi says simply.

'No, I don't.'

'You said –'

'I never tried it, is what I said.'

'Sit down, I'll get you something.' Grace whips up a meal for Stevie and Vi. Vi plays with Ben the dog. Patrick catalogues some CD's and stores them alphabetically in his wiggly chrome CD rack.

'Parmesan cheese on your spaghetti?' Grace offers.

Vi takes the steaming plate. 'Dad says they squeeze it up.'

'Squeeze it up?'

'From overdates supermarket cheddar.'

'Why doesn't that surprise me?'

Soon Stevie has a spaghetti-sauce smile from ear to ear. When at last they hand her the plates, Grace eyes Vi. 'Help me wash up?'

In the kitchen Grace turns to face her. 'Well?'

'Like I need his permission to visit you.'

'Nick's?'

'No, Patrick's. "Would you like to tell us what this is about?"' Vi mimics Patrick's clipped vowels.

'Won't be long till Solly. Then we can picnic together ...'

'Thought you and Patrick were going away.'

'Skiing. Next week. Reward for that piece about BluShield.'

'What piece about BluShield?'

'Transport of hazardous materials, pollutants in rivers, the whole can of worms.'

Grace and Nick, not only separated, but on different sides of the BluShield debate. You made a documentary. Thanks for telling me, Mum.

Vi stacks plates by the sink. 'Know how much BluScreen costs to make? *Less than half a Net credit a metre.*'

'Is this about Nick on TV?'

'He's been like a bear with a sore head.'

'Since the BluShield thing?'

'Since forever. He shoots B12 instead of eating. We only ever meet in the cabbage patch, maybe cook one meal a month. I had berries and rice last week, plus sometimes he makes ice cream. He palms me off with credit cards in place of attention, plus when I went out he cut up my frogs —'

'Is that what you want, a regular dad?'

'Someone who knows what day it is would be nice.'

'Nick knows what day it is.'

'When he isn't studying his blood, like Count Drogo or something.'

'What do you mean?'

'Deep-field blood work. He does it most nights. Takes samples from anyone he can get hold of.'

'Count Drogo,' Patrick opines from the doorway, 'is, I think, King of the Vampyres, a character in a *game* —'

'You mean you Quest half your life.'

'Correct.'

'No time-checks or proper meals.'

'Bingo.'

'He doesn't check your College results?'

'He fixed me self-defence lessons.'

'Did he check out the teacher first?'

'He checked out the teacher's DNA. I had some skin tissue under my nails, and we checked it under the 'scope ...'

'That's it. No more.' Grace raises a hand to block out Ken Wen's DNA, and Vi knows a line has been crossed.

It was this way when Grace walked out. When the last promises to give up the booze had been made, and broken, and remade, and broken again, and that last little drink had tipped the balance, and Grace's face had closed against Nick, Vi had known that that was the end. Never again would her parents live together. Then almost immediately, Nick had jumped on the wagon, and had been on it ever since. Sober now, the oldest schoolboy in the world, with a craggy, world-weary face, still hung up on chemistry experiments, to his credit, he's nothing like Patrick. Suddenly Vi sees how much of her strength she owes to him, how wide he's made her world. The knowledge gives her the strength to get up. 'And anyway, I'm going to bed.'

'Poor frog. You must be tired.'

'You won't tell him what I said?'

'Course not. Of course I won't ...'

They hug for a moment, but betrayal is moments away. As soon as Vi has gone to her room, Grace will chew it over with Patrick. Patrick will nod and agree in a deep and reasonable voice. Then tomorrow, Grace will call Nick and skin him alive in a furious whisper, the only escape from which, as from the rows of yesteryear when they all lived together, will be a deep and immersive game of *QuestHolme* that will hopefully last for days ...

Vi goes to bed at her mother's house feeling bad inside. Shopping Dad, Part Two, has the taste of spaghetti sauce. Still she feels angry with Nick, with the loss of the world outside, connected in her mind with his refusal to see the big picture, BluShield's part in it, his part in BluShield ... The clues to an endless game mill around in her dreams, as though just behind them, tantalizingly almost within reach, lies the sense of it all ...

Violet Niles sits up suddenly in bed at a quarter to two in the morning.

'Reeve?' What time is it? Almost two. Reeve will be Questing with luck. Sometimes you need an ally. Someone to tally your score.

Vi hits Quikdial. 'Reeve, you up?'

'Your mission, should you choose to accept it, is to leave Reeve Dunkley a message,' her answerphone recites.

'Reeve, this is Vi.' The call beams out over microwaves leaping from mast to mast over the desert, entering the watchphone beside Reeve Dunkley's head at precisely one forty-seven a.m. 'I'm over at Mum's house, can't say why, but I need to speak to you soon.' *I'm alone, and in the middle of something big. Nick won't speak to me ever again, once he finds out what I've done. Now I told Mum all these horrible things, I'm not sure exactly why.*

The Vale would love to hear more.

The impossibility of explaining, of passing on something half-suspected in coded language, seems about as impossible as imposing a pattern on her shapeless life with Nick, or on the swimming platelets in a spot of blood under his microscope. Perhaps Reeve will get it anyway, with that perfect sympathy between friends:

'Reeve. You know I'm Blu. Meet me tomorrow. Please.'

'Oh, *what?* We overslept.' The sun is murderously high when Vi parts the curtains next morning. 'Stevie, wake up, it's late.' She flies to the bathroom, bangs on his door.

An odd-looking fledgling chirps on the sill outside the bathroom window. Probably a half-blind thrush, or perhaps a fading blackbird, made stupid by colliding with windows. 'Fly away, birdie, find some shade.' Today of all days, how could they have slept in?

'They've gone,' Stevie says, cereal in hand.

'Grace and Patrick?'

'They left a note. "Off filming after a tip-off."'

'What tip-off?'

'BluShield. Saturday,' Stevie says. 'The biggest scoop of your life.'

Of course.

'My note lay on the mat all night. They must've seen it this morning.'

'Patrick labelled the cereal,' Stevie says. 'Gluten-free or –'

'They must have an hour or two's start on us.'

'I haven't finished my breakfast.'

'The sun's high, it's practically mid-morning – hurry up and get dressed.'

'But –'

'Dress and talk. Suits in the hall. We'll go under sol, for speed.'

'Couldn't they at least have *stopped?* The dead dog in the road has been hit only moments before. Still warm by the time Vi reaches it, the eyes, already cloudy, are glazing already. 'Look what they've done! Don't they *care?*'

A van with the logo NETWORK SEVEN roars off in a cloud of dust.

'Probably he didn't see them,' Stevie says sadly.

'He's blind, can't you see?' UltraViolet jumps up and punches the sky. 'Hit and run, why don't you?'

The Approved off-roader is a speck in the distance by now, the towers of the plastics plant ahead of it framed against the red hills of what was once Two Rivers National Park. Production and Development, BluShield Worldwide, sits on the outskirts of Bayle like the pot of gold at the end of this particular rainbow. One pot of gold that Milt, at least, won't see.

'Sorry, Milt. Hope you get a laser op in the sky.' Vi bends to stroke him, but the body, already stiffening, resists her attempts at comfort. How easy to pour out your heart to a dog. Vi finds the place where the microchip was, now a tiny scar. The place where Sikes shook Milt by the throat. The places the sun must have scorched him, as he padded the desert with Daley. 'I want to bury him.'

'How?'

'At least let's cover him up.'

Gallantly Stevie sweeps off his frilly Blu cloak, torn from the dome at Thoreau. Together they tuck him in at the side of the road. *I'll come back and be your eyes, promise. Tell you what happened at BluShield, everything we saw.*

The body lies in the sand like someone's forgotten parcel. For once UV-B protection is the least and last of Milt's worries. The plastic may flummox the buzzards for a while, but once the sun gets up ...

'What's going on?'

Beyond the buzzards, a commotion builds on the road ahead beneath the distant towers – vehicles, dust-clouds, dark shapes of people gathering – the buzz of something happening.

Stevie shades his eyes. 'I think it may have started.'

'What?'

'Look.' And he gestures ahead.

Chapter 19

BluScreen for Everyone Now

A caterpillar. That's what it is.

'What are they doing?' Vi wonders, as the caterpillar uncurls over the desert, waving its many-legged head.

'Outing BluScreen, what do you think?' Stevie's eyes shine with excitement.

'I thought it would be a protest.'

'No, you didn't.'

In Stevie's eyes is reflected the incredible confusion of the scene outside BluShield Worldwide.

The caterpillars multiply as they watch.

Three − four rolls of BluScreen, streaming out over the desert from the open mouth of warehouse three, as fast as teams of Leakers can seize the ends of the plastic and run with it over their heads. Vi shades her eyes. What a scene! The BluScreen caterpillars doubling back on themselves, coaxing more Blu from the warehouse; more caterpillars starting out, like grubs just hatched in the darkness, unreeling sheets of plastic making Blu the faces beneath them; caterpillars threading in and out of one another, becoming entangled, a criss-cross dance of streaming blue plastic and people determined to celebrate.

'Phoo – *wee!*' Stevie whistles.

'Making a party of it.'

'They waited long enough.'

The Big Out. This is it. The fence has long been trampled, the warehouse doors thrown wide. Five – six caterpillars of snaking, shining BluScreen, prancing and unfolding over the desert with a hundred multicoloured legs, like Chinese carnival dragons.

'So many people,' Vi marvels.

'The Out's huge. Daley's been planning it for weeks.'

'But breaking in – and stealing?'

'They stole the technology to make it.'

'Who from?'

'Everyone.'

'Daley says.'

Vi spots Daley himself at the head of the longest caterpillar, the sun flashing off its long back of winding Blu. Actions, not words, its dance seems to say. Simple! Brave! Real! They must have rolled out the plastic at dawn, been having a ball ever since.

BluScreen For Everyone Now! Signs and placards everywhere. Pictures of children on the fence. **BluScreen! Out! Now!**

'Amazing,' Vi says.

'Isn't it?'

But they don't have it all their own way, once BluShield Security close in. A knot of blue-uniformed guards hustles a figure through the crowd. The sun flashes off two long muzzles

'What's he got?'

'Laser-shears?' Stevie guesses.

Protected by BluShield Security, the figure with laser-shears moves to the mouth of the warehouse, and the roots of the tongues of Blu. The crowd falls back. Re-groups. Without surprise, Vi sees that the figure is Smiley. 'What will he do?'

'Cut the BluScreen, if he can,' someone next to her reckons.

'Isn't it too expensive?'

'They'll ruin it, if they have to.'

Vi turns. 'Mum.'

The giveaway is the van lettered NETWORK SEVEN. Network researcher Grace Evans turns to her daughter thoughtfully. 'Thought you were in bed.'

'You had a tip-off.'

Grace looks at her. 'You?'

Around the stalemate over the laser-shears a crowd mills in odd bits of Protective clothing – ex-company employees, Thoreau freaks, residents of Bayle. Through them a man shoulders a bulky camera.

'Michael! Michael!' Grace spots her cameraman at last. 'Over here!'

Michael the cameraman joins them. 'Sorry we're late. Accident with a dog.'

'This is my daughter. Say Hi. Vi got the tip-off somehow. I sent digital pictures already – newsroom went wild.'

'They scrambled us at seven,' Michael says. Vi looks at him with hate. 'Then we hit some mutt in the road. Almost rolled the rig.'

Why tip me off this morning, and not last night? What's your involvement in this? Just what are you doing here? None of these parental concerns cross Grace Evans's mind. Instead she squeezes Vi's hand. 'My big break – because of you.'

Violet Niles hates her mother sometimes. But not as much as the crowd appears to hate Solar Adviser Smiley and his laser-shears, wielded on BluShield's behalf, and blocked by protesters' bodies throwing themselves over the Blu. The situation looks threatening. Then a posse of bodyguards appears at the gates. A spokesman prepares to speak.

'Any comment on the issues behind the protest?' Grace Evans appears with a microphone saying SEVEN.

'The situation is this.' The spokesman brings out a statement. 'Should those responsible for breaking into the premises of BluShield WorldWide now force the company to destroy its own property by cutting any rolls of Protective, the company will have no hesitation in adding to a charge of Breaking and Entering, a charge of Criminal Damage –'

'BluScreen for Everyone!' Daley starts. In moments the chant is strong. 'BluScreen – Out – Now!' The spokesman brings down his arm, and Smiley brings down his shears. Keen as a knife through butter, the laser cuts through the plastic and a caterpillar falls away. Smiley moves on to the next one. One by one, the lines of protesters collapse as the tails of the caterpillars are severed at the mouth of the warehouse. BluSecurity surround them and try to roll up the BluScreen before they can carry it off.

'Any organization claim responsibility?' Grace follows the spokesman insistently.

'Random Squires!' someone shouts.

'How about Random Squires?'

'Our media consultant, Doctor Nick Niles, is on his way. Until then, no further comment.' The spokesman retreats. The gates close. The battle is only beginning.

BluScreen for Everyone! Now! Vi watches in disbelief as a free-for-all for BluScreen begins. A woman wraps her child in Blu; a dog is tossed into the air as elderly ladies from Bayle tug a length from side to side. A man with a pitted face screams from the back of the crowd: 'I worked for BluShield for thirty years *and I never had compensation!*'

Still Smiley wields his laser-shears. Still the smell of burning tinges fantastic scenes of bodies muddled with plastic, tearing, twisting, tugging, everyone determined, at least, to take home enough Blu to cover a small square of garden. Four caterpillars gone – five. Smiley's laser whines in the sun. His Smart Shades tell him he's had enough UV as he moves on to caterpillar six. BluSecurity roll up what's left. Protesters begin to disperse.

'Wait till the newsroom gets this,' Grace gloats.

'Shouldn't you interview someone from the Out?' Vi worries. A flood of available plastic. The biggest car boot in the world – but what will it look like on television? 'Get the other side of the story?'

'I don't think we need go over the top.'

'You don't know why they're protesting.'

'These pictures tell their own story.'

'But maybe they'll edit them out.'

'I didn't tell Patrick a thing about our little talk last night.' Grace's face looks strange. 'You trust me, don't you?'

What are you talking about? Vi passes a hand over her eyes. Mild sunstroke or what? Roddy Meakin appears in the crowd – Roddy – wait! Daley spins by, his eyes wild and Thrace in his hair, a stinging foam listed in the *Sol* under 'Crowd Control & Its Effects'. Vi feels her head – no foam. Smiley looms up, laser humming, zeroing in on Danny Jope.

'Stop – No! What are you doing?'

Smiley smiles: 'Aren't you in breach of a Confining order?'

'You sent me out to get fried in a leaky suit –'

'Lovely smile. Sunny side up.'

'The sun's quite harmless really.' Reeve pops up in an SAS suit. She dangles a broken leg, horribly twisted and mangled. 'It's easy to be an Adviser. You just take a simple test.'

'What happened to your leg?' Vi reels away. 'I can't believe you're an Adviser –'

'I'd Advise *you* to sit down,' Reeve tells her gravely.

'Meet me at a secret destination,' Stevie the Face chips in. 'Don't forget those last-minute things –'

A trailer parts the crowd and Doctor UV climbs out. Waving, he throws down parasols made of BluScreen, like the Mother Teresa of plastic. Milt the blind dog appears at his feet, only very slightly battered from the accident that killed him. Then something unravels inside Vi's mind.

Milt was dead.

Now he's not.

'What a *good idea* these parasols are,' Grace reports to camera.

'Go ahead, take one.' Nick looms, suddenly close. 'Take one, it means you choose me.'

'Choose me!' Grace reaches out to her pathetically. Picnics. Warmth. Believe me.

The parasol trembles between them in Nick's hand. *Choose me. No, me.* Daley, where are you? So much depends upon a Blu parasol. Glinting with sunshine. Against the yellow desert. Glowing radiation from the sun glances off it, she can *see* the UV-B now. The handle of the parasol glows. Every little detail, showing exactly the way it's made.

Violet Eveline Niles puts out her hand.

Me! No, me!

'I'll take that.' A hand closes over the parasol. 'Maybe a little late,' says Headingley, 'but I think I can use one of these.' She snaps it up over her sun-blasted face. Takes a look at the crowd. 'What are you all doing here? Don't you know the sun's bad for your health?'

'Would you like a carrot?' Bruce Stallingham pops up, his face unreasonably large. 'I'm afraid I haven't peeled them. Would you like a carrot? I'm afraid I haven't —'

UltraViolet holds her head. Something hard and bulky

over her ears, something over her eyes. It doesn't make sense, please stop!

'Would you like to give someone else a turn?'

'*Shut up and leave me alone!*'

'Now, that's not nice.' A BluSecurity guard looms before her, his Tenth Dynasty wicker armour creaking as he draws his sword. Vi takes up a defensive posture. He throws the Dragon; Vi counters with the Snake, a twisting throw that takes her opponent over her shoulder, his face *the face of Ken Wen*. He springs up; tries the Ox, a full-bodied charge. As UltraVi fells him with the Wen Chop his cry sounds a lot like someone –

'*Violet! Stop! You're hurting me!*'

– she knows. Something tears around her eyes, and suddenly daylight floods in. The lights, at least, of a bedroom somewhere.

And she's in her room.

Fighting someone. Across the floor lies a trail of objects, a parasol, poster, camera, staple gun, rubber caterpillar. Some Questgame runs on the walls, degrading into muddy colours.

Nick sits up. In his hand, the headset he ripped off her head. 'Thank God for that.'

While aghast in the door stand Abby and a boy she half-knows called Rawley. And Rawley's eyes say, Unreal, will you look at *that*!

Chapter 20
Inside, Looking Out

The tray of objects looks as suggestible as usual. 'Staple gun suggested the laser-shears, maybe. Or actually the dressmaking scissors?' Nick points them out. 'You say the parasol's pretty obvious, but the carrot?'

'Part of an earlier level.' Violet remembers it now. The trip to Brucie's house. Or was that part of reality? 'You mean, the Out *never happened?*'

'You might need some time to think about it.'

'But Afterminster —'

'Not even in the gameplan. C'mon, you know that's not real.'

Closing her eyes, Vi feels the objects on the tray. Even a NetCredit card. 'You treated me to Edition Eight — that happened, didn't it?'

'*QuestHolme Futures*, enhanced graphics,' Nick nods.

'So why did the game degrade?'

'Sustain your own storylines. Depends on what you put in.'

'Clues, you mean?'

'Gameplans. Moving characters around.'

Gameplans triggered by feelies. A dog's collar. Even a bag of Power Mix. One of those parasols Nick once designed, that had hung in her room ever since BluShield had rejected it as making the product too *available*. Were these pathetic bits and pieces really the stuff of the drama still playing inside her mind? Direct to Net. Violet Life. All Sagittarians this week. Don't try reading these horrorscopes any more. I can't see beyond next week. Was the Out nothing but a game? Just a *QuestHolme Future?*

'One of a number of possible Futures actually,' Nick comments.

'Sorry, I'm thinking aloud. I can't tell what's inside or outside my mind these days.'

Nick nods. 'Seems there's a limit.'

'A limit to what?'

'Tolerance of games like *QuestHolme.* When games are so convincing you invest your feelings in them, that's the point at which you need to stop.'

'I Quested you lost your job. Handed out parasols instead.'

'Could be self-fulfilling.'

'Why?'

'Quit my job.'

'You *resigned?*'

'Called BluShield when I got in.'

'Got in, when?'

Nick shrugs. 'Which "when" would you like?'

214

Abby enters with a tray of tea, sets it down, and tactfully withdraws. 'Anything you want at Wesley? Silly question.'

How has she not noticed how nice Abby is? Vi feels adrift on a sea with new landmarks, things she sees more clearly even without fancy contacts, some things only glimpsed, others staring her in the face …

'And I've been Questing since when?'

'Since I bought you the New Edition.'

'Seemed so real.'

'That's the Quest.'

'I never did get all the clues …'

'Says here,' Nick checks the Guidebook, 'the identity of "Random Squires" is the key to level eighty-nine.'

'But Random Squires is real. He customized the Quest.'

'Maybe they employ him now.'

'He writes for the *Sol*. Posters tunnels – he's everywhere.'

'People need hero figures. He doesn't exist.'

People need heroes. *You gave up your job.* Vi considers Nick. 'How's the arm?'

'You pack a punch.'

'A Snake, actually.'

'Could have done without the chop to the legs.'

'I thought you were a Tenth Dynasty warrior, mixed up with a security guard and my self-defence instructor.'

'It's obvious how that could happen.'

'You should have resisted me with your *Ki*.'

'Fresh out of *Ki*, I'm afraid.'

Behind Nick the muddled screens of the Quest melt into gentle loops on the quietening walls of Vi's room. A samurai charges Nick, but falls down before he arrives. Without the imagination to sustain its own past or future, the undirected game approaches meltdown.

'I can't believe I just gamed the summer away.'

'Plenty of time left.'

'I meant to go outside.'

'Still can.'

'I blame the parents.'

'Me too.'

The menu for *QuestHolme Futures* briefly appears. Copyright Squires Corps 2020. Running down now into a muddy loop, how could anyone have seen it as a substitute for smelly, glorious, disappointing, thrilling life?

'Anyway, I'm out of a job.'

'Over me?'

'Over everything.' The look in Nick's eyes takes in the last few extraordinary weeks, Vi's gaming, his crisis of conscience – everything that's happened.

Vi watches him. 'How do you feel?'

Nick nods slowly. 'Free.'

'What will we do?'

'Raise frogs.'

'Excuse me?'

'Amphibian repopulation, it's going to be huge.'

'You can make parasols.'

'Not bad.'

'Abby can market them.'

'Now you're going too far.'

'How about doing picnics?'

'Picnics?'

'A walk on the wild side. Everything You Need to go Out. Hamper, rug, sun-block, dog …'

'… ants and sandy sandwiches.' Nick throws back his head and laughs. 'I make a mean salad torpedo. You know, I think I could do it. And talking of picnics …'

'What is it?'

'Your mother called. She wants to take you out.'

'This afternoon?'

'Better put these away.' Nick weighs the headsets in his hands. He looks up with a question in his eyes. 'Unless you think she might be late.'

Chapter 21

Blu————————————

'They're relaxing rads. I want to take you outside.'

'Are you serious? I mean, why would they?' Violet Niles meets Grace Evans over a Minster Mall Special Offer Coffee. Her mother's eyes watch hers over a cappucino moustache. Around them, the bustle of people out enjoying themselves in summer clothing too tight for them is cooled by the vents thrown open on to a warming, but not-too-hot day.

'Seems we have a little protection this year.'

'More ozone?'

'More Blu.'

'Less sunshine at last,' a woman nods, in passing.

'Lovely day,' Vi responds.

It is a lovely day, isn't it? Mild for the time of year. Lovely weather. Set to stay. Cloudy enough for you? Vi rehearses the rusty phrases that people are beginning to exchange once again, in the unusually clement weather. The forecast gives out 'overcast' until at least the middle of next week. 'And clement into next week, with some cloud formations giving us these pleasant, late-summer skies ...'

Clement's a nice word. Gentle, merciful, mild. Seems the

sun's strength has mellowed for a while, due to slower formation of ozone-destroying clouds. Surprising what comes out when the sun goes in.

How are you? How's the family? Haven't seen you for a while! Neighbours hail one another across the Minster Mall, its tea-garden filled with shoppers, mums, dads, families, its thatched eating area and half-timbered walls reminding Vi of Afterminster, though the cosy past time she imagines she remembers has more to do with the warmth in Grace Evans's eyes.

'Those things I said about Dad …'

'What things?'

'Oh, you know. He ignores me. He's irresponsible. Emphasising all the bad things, without saying how brisk he is.'

'I know. You're cross about Patrick.'

'That obvious?' UltraViolet sees over-clever Patrick in the shine in her mother's eyes. Sees him scornfully sweeping out of the house. Looking down his nose, but never looking back. 'Boyfriends come and go, but family's here for always.'

'I should be telling you that.'

'Can I stay as long as I like?'

'Long as you like. Patrick's away.'

'Just you and me then.'

''Fraid so.'

Quality time together at last. If only all problems were as simple as getting rid of Patrick for a while. 'Can we go to the beach sometime soon?'

'Afraid we'll have to do whatever we like.'

'I've wasted so much time playing games.'

'We've all had cabin-fever, I think.' Grace snaps up a parasol. 'Thank God for Parascreens – ready?'

Between them they swing a picnic hamper out on to the balmy boulevards, freshly planted with trees.

'Will there be warm cucumber sandwiches?' Vi feels the wind on her face.

'And smelly boiled eggs? Of course.'

On their way past Reeve's house they bump into Roddy Meakin twirling a clement parasol himself. The idea of going for a walk, formerly a no-no, is now catching on really fast.

'Dig the Limited Edition,' UltraVi compliments him.

Roddy gives it a twirl. The maker's instructions read: *Dr UV's ParaScreens. 100% Blu-thene. 99.9 % protection against UV-A and B. Do not leave closed in full sol.*

'Bat the Toad, in silver. I queued for this baby three hours.'

Only five hundred Parascreens have a Questcharacter in silver. That was part of the deal, and Violet's own idea. Limited editions had to convert Questheads like Roddy, too brisk to go outside, too cool to carry anything *para* – against, *sol* – the sun.

Unless, that is, parasols were brisk.

Now the new parasols are everywhere, since old stocks of prototype BluScreen, bought up by Nick Niles some time ago and kept ever since in his garage, have been manufactured into a range of brisk, deep, sunshades on the theme of Questcharacters. It wasn't hard to tie in with the

Squires Corps, the company behind the Quest, to promote a truly clement way to stay safe and cool in the sun. Seems they were waiting for a way to bring the Quest outside, since the parents of every pallid Questhead blamed the Squires Corps for a lack of sociability. Once BluShield lost the court case, they couldn't do anything about it.

The parasols would be called *Parascreens*, and would be easily affordable to everyone. Now BluShield lost its patents on BluScreen, anyone can borrow the formula. Blu-thene belongs to everyone. You can make your own parasol. Decorate your garden with waving banners of Protective. Go out whenever you want.

'My idea to make Limited Editions,' Vi lets Roddy know.

'Can you get me a silver Seshwan?'

'Squires Corporation decides when Silvers come out.'

'You don't have anything to do with it?'

'I helped make the ads.'

'Actually film them?'

Vi nods. 'The one where Stevie says: "Face, here. Always clement outside with Doctor UV's Parascreens." And there's a shot of Stevie's face in the rain. Parasols falling like leaves, and he says: "Go outside and catch one. Log off – go out – tune in." – "tune in" was Dad's idea.'

'And the Questcharacters?'

'My idea too.'

Roddy nods. 'Clement. I'm trading Guardians from Usher Wood for *any Dragon King* from the Japanese cycle. Make up a set, if I can get one.'

Vi eyes him through Bat the Toad. Roddy Meakin, not

only carrying, but trading, parasols. Did she get it right, or what? 'Henchmen are trading fast. So are Count Drogos.'

'Drogos are everywhere.'

'Not the Day-Glo kind.'

'There's Day-Glo Drogos?' Roddy gapes.

'Jamie Steele's got one.'

'What about Seshwans?'

'Just out.'

'Later.' Rodders heads off in a quest for parasols decorated with Day-Glo 'Emperor Seshwans' to get one over on Jamie Steele. He'll join the waiting list. Be a hundred and ninth.

Log off — go out — tune in.

The television ads are brisk, and have somehow caught the mood. *Always clement, with Doctor UV.* Stevie's face in the rain, raindrops falling like forgiveness over the woods and fields; Stevie's eyes opening, a peerless brown like Vi's, underneath those contacts. *All the smells of summer with Parascreen Protection.* The other ad features Nick Niles himself: *Experience the world outside with portable UV-exclusion. All it takes is the 'Quit' option.*

Now that 'blu-thene' costs a fraction of what it did as BluScreen, outside *is* for everyone. So the world turns Blu. That patched old greenhouse at Thoreau can be swapped for a gleaming dome as smooth as Harty-Noakes's head. Even the black spider of Condorcet may throw on a gleaming Blu skin, the tunnels linking gardens together until they 'roll' for Winter Solstice, or maybe stay permanently linked. They even started a Public Parasol scheme, with Doctor UV's blessing. Borrow a parasol from any public stand in town, pop it back when you're finished. So a wash of Blu travels around town and extends to the Undercliff, where on Hume Island, for the first time since Victorian days, a new herd of goats has appeared ...

'Isn't that Danny Jope?'

'What's he doing – dancing?' Grace squints at a capering figure ahead. 'That boy had the jackpot out of the fruit machine at Mister Kidney's in less than ten minutes last night – a hundred and fifty Credits, they'd tried for months before that.'

Vi shakes her head. 'What is he like.'

The figure of what appears to be Danny Jope swings around a radon-meter, high and dry since its tunnel Rolled. Parasol in hand, Jope is actually busking. The all-singing, all-dancing model is a hit with passing oldies, who shell out NetCredits happily for *Singin' in the Sun*.

I'm singin' in the sun –

Just singin' in the sun –

What a glorious feeling –

My LIFE has begun –

'Sure you've got the words right?' Vi laughs.

Jope leaps on and off the kerb. Grass is actually sprouting in the gaps between kerbstones, now that the removal of the tunnel lets the pavement breathe.

I'm laughing at clouds –

With a hap-hap-happy something something –

Cos I'm singin' – and dancin' – in the sun –

Dooby-doo-doo, dooby-dooby-doo-doo ...

Old ladies are actually dancing arm-in-arm in the park adjacent to Jope's pitch. All along the Boulevard with its blooming trees and orange-juice stalls, its 'Tunnels Out of Use' signs and airy cafes, people exchange the time of day and try to remember how to feed the ducks on the newly blu-thened pond. Not a person in the park without a parasol, they paint a Blu and moving scene not easily forgotten.

'Fifty-four Credits, not bad.' Jope collects his hat.

'When was the last time I saw you?' Vi wonders aloud.

'Dunno.'

'You Quest much this summer?'

'You?'

'More than I meant to.'

'When we brought some slides for the doc.'

'What?'

'Roddy and me. Last time we saw you. At your house.'

With an effort Vi remembers her guests. So long ago now, she'd left them gaming in her room to cut up some lengths of BluScreen for a suit, desperate to get outside, a suit that would go well now in a museum, labelled 'Suit Made When Blu Was Valuable'.

'You're wrong,' says Vi. 'We met at Wesley since then. You told me about your brother –'

'Guess what? Daley came home.'

Vi flushes. 'That's good.'

'He doesn't stay, but he visits. He tells me all this Leaker stuff. Doing anything, Tuesday? You can meet him if you want.'

'Is there a blind dog with him?'

'How did you know?'

'What will he do?'

'Lie around and eat.'

'Daley, I mean.'

'Study stuff on Tibet.'

'At the explorer's house?'

'You know about Thoreau?'

Vi licks her lips. 'He use the name "Random Squires"?'

'When he writes for the *Sol*, why not?'

As easy as that. Mystery solved.

'Rolling the tunnels early,' Jope chats as they walk along.

'Solly in only three weeks,' Vi agrees. 'Seems too good to be true.'

They stop before they reach the corner where Grace Evans tactfully waits.

Jope picks up on the rug and hamper. 'Picnic?'

'No prizes.'

'Undercliff?'

'Uh-huh.'

'My sister would have liked to have come.'

'Your sister?'

'Her name was Mary Louise,' Danny says. 'Dad called her Dolly Daydreams. I don't remember her much.'

'Dolly Jope? You mean she's *real*?'

'She kept running out to the Undercliff. Like I say, I don't remember.'

In your own time! Grace Evans waves on the corner. For once, Vi's foresight deserts her. She can't 'see' 'Dolly' Jope

225

at all − no pictures, no feelings, no memories. 'I have to go.'

'Yeah.' Jope understands.

'Say Hi to Jamie if you see him.'

'Tomorrow. We're all going out. Meet us in town, if you want.'

The notion of casually meeting friends in town warms Vi's mind like the memory of regular meals, cosy towels on the beach.

'Afternoon's ticking away.'

'Sorry.' Vi takes up her side of the picnic hamper, rejoining Grace, mind racing. *So Daley went home and kept his side of the bargain. Doing anything Tuesday?* Perhaps he comes into town. His brother is only a part of his life. The rest lies at Thoreau. Expect 'Random Squires' to write about Tibet in the *Sol* from the sun-flooded Study under Harty-Noakes's pipe-rack, a dozing Milt at his side ...

'Here's Reeve.' Grace greets her.

'I've seen so many people I know, takes me all morning to do the shopping,' Reeve says breezily.

'Everyone's out and about. How are you, Reeve?'

'Clement.'

'That word again. Take the hamper, will you?'

Vi and Reeve share the load. They fall into step together. Slowly. It's been so long.

'How's the ankle?'

'Fine.'

'I Quested you broke your leg. That's before the game degraded.'

226

'Having trouble?'

Vi nods. 'Futures, Edition Eight.'

'Questing all summer?'

'On and off – you?'

Reeve shrugs. 'Confining Order.'

'I think I had one too.'

'Amnesty now, anyway. All rads back to four, no matter what you've got.'

'How will that work?'

'Universal Protection under Blu.'

'Clement.'

'Well clement.'

'You bought a Sol.'

'Why not?'

'So is Smiley good or bad?'

'Take a look at the headline. What do you think?'

Davis Nailey Exclusive – Sacked Adviser Blows Whistle on Central Advice Link to Vale. PLUS '*BluShield Ruined My Health and I Had No Compensation*', an ex-worker speaks. PLUS Win Yourself a Limited Edition Silver Seshwan, in Competition of the Year!

'I can never make up my mind about him.' Vi hands back the magazine.

'He used us to get back into the system.'

'You remember all that – the Glade?'

'In Quest-time.'

'You mean –'

Reeve shakes her head sympathetically. 'You think you're the only one with Edition Eight links to the Net?'

'But I direct the game.'

'Only your part of it. I joined you in the guest room. All the others were there.'

'What, my mother?'

'Home scenarios do have them.'

'But he did send me out in a leaky suit –'

'And Stallingham – ''

'Did go to hospital.'

'But if the Glade's in Quest-time …'

'Don't even go there,' Reeve says. 'What's real anyway?'

They pick up the pace, the hamper bumping between them. Vi's mind is in a whirl. 'I went to find him too, but he wasn't there.'

'Smiley?'

Vi brings out a Sol. **'Hume Island Special'**, the headline reads.

'Not another desert island thing.'

'They're going to start a community.'

'Only Leakers and flakes need apply,' Reeve says sardonically.

'Headingley's in it. They're making a dome. Taking goats across.'

'Oh dear.'

'At least it's real.'

'At least.' Reeve meets Vi's eyes over the hamper. 'This picnic – can I come?'

They swing along together easily, in rhythm now, ripples

of half-remembered outings in every creak of the wicker bumping along between them. *Of all the people we met today, you're the one I want to come.*

'I thought,' says UltraViolet, 'you were never going to ask.'

Chapter 22

Hume————————

A single song-thrush on a May bough pours out its heart on the breeze, its throat throbbing with the notes that soar out over the sunny air like the very voice of summer ...

'Intense,' UltraViolet breathes.

Still the Undercliff sleeps under its crags, just the way she remembered it. Beneath its wooded gullies Hume Island can be glimpsed through the trees, late summer foliage cloaking its coves and inlets. The soft crash of the waves below gives a drowsy feel to the sheltered air and a salt smell to the breeze whenever a break in the tree-cover shows the edge of the cliff.

'Here?' Vi suggests as a clearing offers, very green and very soft. They lower the hamper between them. Already rooks scold overhead, indignant that someone should come here. Grace puts her hands on her hips. 'What a fuss they make. They can't have it all to themselves.'

'We came here before,' Reeve says. 'Remember the giant rhubarb?'

The huge, barbed stems with their leathery leaves

remind Vi of a giant's pie, mixed-up scale, freaky things, when everything needs to be normal. 'What are those red things?'

'Flowers maybe?' Reeve goes over and touches one. Hairy red flower-bodies of some kind, each the size of a head, sit at the base of each stem.

'Flowers that look like heads?'

'Gunnera,' her mother says crisply, in her television researcher's voice. 'Originates from Japan. It's a garden escape.'

The leathery leaves of the Gunnera knock gently together in the breeze that rushes through the Hart's Tongue ferns, like the whisper of their coming. Who's on the island? whispers the breeze ...

'Hume.' Vi takes a look at its crazily tilted slopes through the trees. 'It's a bit of the cliff, isn't it?'

'Huge landslip,' Grace nods. 'One stormy night in 1863. Next morning, there it was – a new island.'

Hume looks new again today, under a clement sun. A new island in an old sea. Ready for plants to colonize.

Who's on the island?

A fleeting figure in something red. UltraVi blinks and it's gone.

'There's someone there.'

'On the island?'

'No one there now,' Grace says.

'There is,' puts in Reeve. 'Isn't there?'

'A new community or something,' Vi says. 'I'm starving. Can we eat?'

After salad and rolls and a strange, crusty cake contributed by Nick, 'Frogs!' Grace suddenly remembers.

'Not for me,' Reeve says.

'Nick dropped them off with the cake.' Grace rips a hole-studded lid off another container. 'They look as though they're ready.'

The world of tiny frogs inside smells fishy and looks distressed.

'I should have remembered.' Vi looks in. 'He's right, it's time to release them.'

They finish with flapjack and apples, and after a while they grow quiet. Reeve yawns and stretches luxuriously on the grass. Above her the leaves make a fretwork against the sky, letting in occasional shafts of sunlight.

'Pass me my Approveds, will you?'

Vi hands over Reeve's sunglasses. 'Going to find a place for the frogs,' she says, taking up their container.

'Mind the edge,' Grace warns. 'Remember Mary Jope.'

Vi takes an inbreath. 'What happened to Mary Jope?'

'Only six. Wouldn't stay indoors. Whether she tried to climb down the cliff and got caught by the tide at the bottom, or what she tried to do –'

Only one way down from the Undercliff, and that's a dive into the sea. Was it Headingley who said that?

'Some say she reached Hume Island, so at least she did escape somehow. That's what they said when they found her in the sea – doesn't Danny ever mention it?'

'Says he doesn't remember her much.'

232

'Don't suppose he does. Elder brother never got over it. Ran away eventually, never heard of since.'

'Daley's back, didn't you know?'

'I never really knew them that well. Place makes you sleepy, doesn't it?' Grace yawns mightily. 'Don't get lost then.'

'I won't.'

Suddenly the spell of the Undercliff feels more dangerous than it did. UltraViolet plunges away with a racing heart. Little Mary Jope, floating in the sea with her arms outstretched and her hair washing gently around her. Vi can see her now. Don't dilly-dally, 'Dolly' Jope. Race through the undergrowth, brambles clawing your legs, in a desperate bid for freedom. Had she had the blue eyes of a Daley? Impossible to guess. Would she rather have died outside than live a prisoner of the sun any longer, in the gloom of her darkened room? Had her death inspired Daley to run away too? Made him the embodiment of 'Random Squires', striker-out for freedom?

Vi walks on through the trees, and the hush settles around her and calms her. Birds flicker and whirr; a jewelled dragonfly hovers; ferns and creepers tickle her legs, butterflies surprise her. Tantalizing glimpses of Hume wink at her through the trees. Emerging at last on to that bare nose of limestone, the Beak, Vi sees it clearly below her.

Hume Island, so near you could touch it.

And on it, a lonely figure. A goat or two picks its way over the rocks above it.

The lonely figure waves.

Vi waves back impulsively. *Mary Jope! In your dungarees! You did escape after all!*

A cloud dims the glare of the sun. Vi's gaze clears. As a shadow races over her, the girl on Hume is revealed, not as some little ghost, after all, but as someone she knows very well. As if she'd known it all along, she sees that the figure is Headingley.

Bo Headingley waves again. Cups her mouth. Points at something above her.

'Major rhubarb!' Vi shouts back. And above her the Gunnera nods.

The figure of Headingley waves once more, then winks away on a path. Vi follows her red T-shirt through the green. The ghost of a dog leaps beside her – Sikes, unTagged and free! Bo Headingley looks happy, the first of a new community, leading away her fresh herd of goats to join those still surviving on the island, her T-shirt and dungarees flashing away in the trees.

UltraVi watches her go. *Who's on the island?* the wind through the Undercliff whispers. *Headingley, Dolly, Mary – real or not, past or future?*

Real. And very now. Smiley's probably there too. Good luck to 'em, Vi decides, the wind filling her lungs and hair, the waves foaming way below. UltraViolet, not sheathed in BluScreen for once, with your hair and clothes streaming in the wind, at the highest point of the cliff! A moment wholly your own! Tearing off her Approveds on an impulse, she throws the sunglasses away from her into a long arc over the sea ...

234

*

Violet Niles opens her hand and a tiny frog jumps out of it. Sand and dirt immediately clings to its skin. Vi fights an urge to help it and reaches for another. The second frog has to be pushed. Once on the grass it blinks, swallows, turns; then springs! And springs! And springs!

Deciding at last to release them near a little gushing spring, and afraid of hurting them, she tips the rest of them out on to a stone. Within minutes the miniature frogs begin to disperse, some immediately gone in the stream, others hesitant in the grass. One of them finds Vi's toes. She shakes it off – Go, there's a world out there! – and in wanting it to go, yet being unable to take her eyes off it, feels strangely what parents must feel like.

Some time later, filled with coolness and green-ness, Vi returns to the picnic.

Grace looks up from a book. 'Nice walk?'

'Excellent.'

'Those guys get away OK?'

Vi upends the container. 'They looked so tiny and vulnerable. Hope some of them survive.'

'Odds-on they live to be forty.'

'Frogs don't live to be forty.'

'Those are the ones you don't see.'

'Someone on the island!' Reeve points from a rock.

'What does he think he's doing?' Grace gets up.

Vi discerns a dark form. 'That's a man called Davis Nailey.'

'You know him?'

'Smiley – making a shelter.'

'What for, he won't be able to stay in it.'

'Building for the future, maybe?'

Now they can hear him as the wind swings around, bringing them the *nee-naw* of a saw biting through wood, the tunk-tunk of a hammer on nails, hopeful sounds against the swash of the sea below, triggering memories of home DIY only dimly remembered.

'Hope they make it,' Reeve says.

'I love the wild, not less than the good,' murmurs Grace.

'Tell us then.'

'Who said that? A wild man called Thoreau.'

I see it going well. UltraViolet sees many things, impossible to explain. 'Probably we should go.'

Leaving is so much easier when you know that you can return at any time. But still the mood is sombre as the cool of the evening descends and the path wends quietly homeward. The single day in the life of a dragonfly closes with its fading strength. Birds come out to call the day over.

Now the day is over —

Night is falling nigh —

Shadows of the evening —

Steal across the sky.

The old primary school day-closer seems to be a part of herself. Violet Niles can almost hear the scraping of chairs being lifted on to desks, except it was always cyber-school, never the real thing, except in the very beginning, when she was dimly four — or was that a dream as well? Or was it something Nick told her, from a childhood even longer ago?

Vi shoulders her pack and follows Reeve. Already the streaks of sunset are streaming across the sky as they reach the crest of the path. The burning ball of the sun shimmers on the horizon, over Nailey's Crusoe-like shelter, over Hume itself and the line of the Undercliff fuzzing the division between cliffs and sea with a wavering edge of green far into the distance.

'Beautiful, isn't it? Sometimes I think –' Grace's eyes sweep the horizon – 'if all this dies …'

Violet takes her hand. 'I know what you mean, but it won't.'

Nothing so dramatic. Instead I see life going on – muddly, uncertain, lucky, unlucky – a patchwork of do's and don't's.

Somewhere near the site of the former picnic, on the crushed and imprinted grass, a tiny frog struggles up a twig, throat beating, senses alert, gulping air into its lungs. It feels the strength in its tiny limbs – then springs! And springs! And springs!

Chapter 23
Solly

'Controlled picnics – that's a hopeful sign.'

'Now the sun's not so strong,' Vi agrees, 'soon we'll be able to go anywhere.'

'Can't count on that every year,' Nick says over his microscope.

'And anyway, it's Solly.' UltraViolet drums her feet at the breakfast bar. Only the biggest day of the year. But will he ever look up? 'I can't believe you're not working today.'

'I am working.'

'Telly, I mean.'

'They asked, I said no.'

'Coming out later or what? Street party could be grim, but Jamie and Reeve planned this barbecue –'

'These tardigrades – they're adapting.' Nick looks up at last, a pink pressure ring from the 'scope imprinted around his eye. 'Developing with changing conditions. Take a look at this.'

Reluctantly Vi applies her eye. In the quiet world of the Bears of the Moss under the microscope, tardigrades that look more like caterpillars join and pop out babies. 'They're having babies – so what?'

'The amazing thing is, they can go to sleep, wake up when conditions are right. It's called cryptobiosis. Means they can survive below freezing point, under pressure, in vacuums – resist UV radiation. I left these dishes outside. Now they're waking up under UV-B, reproducing, changing ...'

'Like us, you mean. We live indoors – that's adapting.'

'Let me see the Parachelas, maybe they're doing the same thing.' Switching the dish of 'armoured' Bears for a dish of the non-armoured variety, Nick adjusts his focus.

UltraVi slides away. Looks like he's in for the day. Those tardigrades, they're feisty. Should be in at the end, when the earth falls into the sun. Shifting rooms, the smart walls give her *Good Morning* on channel nine. Jenny of the stiff hair looks as though she's loosened up a little.

'Society adapts to a new way of life, that's what the papers are saying today. More of that later. Meanwhile, Solstice Day kicks off on *Sunspots* with the chance to win Limited Edition Parascreens designed by our own Nick Niles for the first ten correct answers to this question: What is the correct name of the so-called Northern Lights? Is it: a) Aurora Borealis, b) Aurora Australis or c) Aurora Bolognese? Those Limited Edition Silvers are waiting. No "Use Only as Advised" stickers on *these* babies, today of all days, as on the streets this morning the party is just beginning –'

Vi kills the power. Today of all days, let's not stay in and watch television.

*

The girl with the violet eyes saunters down Hobbes and on to Voltaire, the boulevards bright with flags, but as yet deserted. So Solly this year has a little less significance than usual, since everyone went outside anyway, but that's what makes it special – a Solly like no other, since Solstice Day first marked the beginning of winter safety outside, the end of nine months as moles.

That first picnic on the Undercliff had looked forward to the freedoms of Solstice Day. So had the chance to move freely between Bayle and Condorcet, Grace and Nick, for a change – emotional freedom and the space to explore it being a new dot on UltraVi's landscape. So had the trip, under a Parascreen, to the spot where Milton had died.

Except, of course, that he hadn't. The spot on the red dirt road where a Network off-roader had felled him on the day of the Out betrays not a sign of the accident. Vi had promised to come back and be his eyes. But Milt can be seen cheerfully crossing the road with Daley, whenever Daley's in town on supply-duty from Thoreau.

Daley calls in quite a lot now. Tuesdays are a regular thing. Daley and Vi, they hang out. Go out to Thoreau and back, via the Ocean Boulevard, now replanted with rock-daisies – even fly kites on the beach, where Milt always goes in the sea.

So there was no real need, that day, to go sadly together to the place. Milt even lay down on his death-spot till Daley said, Better go. It's only a game, Daley said. But even games tell the truth.

Still the look at the now-defunct BluShield plant had felt exceptionally good. Production has moved to Mirabeau, where cheap and easily-made blu-thene pours out like shiny toffee and is sold on rolls at Wesley, and at every co-operative like it, at a price that will buy you a little of that rare luxury, toilet paper.

Wandering early through Condorcet now, the days seem to blend with one another. Winter solstice, and that time of year when the sun reaches its furthest point south of the equator. Less rays coming in at last. Those UV-B resistant spruces make ideal Christmas trees, with the festive season hard on the heels of Solly, at the same time as unseasonal crocus are showing their heads under blu in gardens everywhere, ready for next spring already. Hard to remember, exactly, when the seasons got mixed up. What to get Patrick for Christmas? How not to spend it beside him? Hello? Where is everyone?

The Hobbes Boulevard stands empty with its flags and waiting tables. In every home the television booms – people staying in to watch 'A Celebration of Solstice Day', while outside the streets are deserted.

At eleven o'clock the party will begin. Even the old and infirm will be wheeled outside to enjoy the fresh air and sunshine. There'll be a barbecue, dancing, hopefully not Morris men. Maybe a silly competition or two, the inevitable men dressed as women, always someone in ducting dressed as a tunnel. Vi can see it already, a Solly to remember, if it would only start and people come outside already, the reason the whole thing got started ...

Who's this coming to meet her, the only hero in town? Could it be that principled man with the craggy face, the one they call Dr ParaScreen?

'Dad!'

UltraViolet walks to meet Nick Niles under a perfect overcast sky. Hobbes Boulevard stretches before her, over-brimming with flowers, even the Minster Mall itself decked with Solly Day streamers. A winter chill in the air, already. Now the sun will subside until the long banks of chlorine-breeding clouds appear over the skyline next January, maybe less, maybe more, next year. Meanwhile out on the Undercliff, twelve out of twenty frogs survive ...

'Dad!'

He sees her at last. As they close the distance between them under the Solly Day flags tearing in the wind, Vi feels as though a tight band is closing around her head.

Vi removes her headset. 'Another silly Future.'

'Bit over the top, I agree.' Nick ducks out of his headset, killing the shared Edition Eight experience a few seconds after Vi. 'The ending's too hurried. As though you need to wrap it up quickly, get everything explained, and get on with some idyllic picnic somewhere, as though the sun's going to go away.'

'And parasols are going to change it.'

'The Dolly Jope thing's quite poignant.'

'Yes, but it's all too complicated. The Random Squires thing is introduced almost as an afterthought, and Smiley – would he build an island community?'

'Should've done more with Headingley.'

'Yes, but she loses her mind. What are you going to do?'

'Something – I don't know.'

'We're supposed to care about the story, but it's just a string of events, not much character development, no humour in it or anything.'

'Bruce and his carrots.'

'That's funny?'

'Slightly ironic maybe. Some nice scenes. I enjoyed Thoreau Place.'

'That's because Thoreau Place is real.'

'The Quest works best with real things worked in. Did you ever find the last clue?'

'When I worked out that Daley was Random Squires, this must have printed out off the Net.' Violet rescues a manuscript from the printer entitled *UltraViolet*. 'I guess it leads back to itself – that's what the guidebook means by "Personalized".'

Nick grins. 'A book. Better than going outside.'

'Anyone can be Random Squires – maybe that's the point.'

'Hero-figures, they're everywhere.'

'I think Dr Parascreen should have given away parasols, not sold them.'

'I donated some for a competition, remember?'

'So will you really?'

'Maybe.'

'Is that a yes?'

'This is the book of the game, remember?'

'At least my fifth different ending.'

'Way to explore your feelings.'

'Thanks for being on my side.'

'There is only one side, isn't there?'

Bing-bong!

Their eyes widen. 'Front door,' Vi says. 'Must be Mum.'

Nick takes the book titled after her. 'Who needs reality when you can read?'

'Or Quest.'

Don't go there, his eyes warn urgently.

'Did you think I would? With Mum waiting outside and winter coming? The beach and the woods to walk in? Daley and me going out?'

'See, now I think you might mean it.'

Handing him the headsets, Vi jumps up to go. 'Put these away for good. Did you think I couldn't do it?' She laughs with delight and amazement at herself. 'UltraViolet, aren't I? Strong enough to crack the Quest. Strong enough to stop.'

www.puffin.co.uk.www.puffin.co.uk.www.puffin.co.uk

bookinfo.competitions.news.games.sneakpreviews

www.puffin.co.uk.www.puffin.co.uk.www.puffin.co.uk

adventure.bestsellers.fun.coollinks.freestuff

www.puffin.co.uk.www.puffin.co.uk.www.puffin.co.uk

explore.yourshout.awards.toptips.authorinfo

www.puffin.co.uk.www.puffin.co.uk.www.puffin.co.uk

greatbooks.greatbooks.greatbooks.greatbooks

www.puffin.co.uk.www.puffin.co.uk.www.puffin.co.uk

reviews.poems.jokes.authorevents.audioclips

www.puffin.co.uk.www.puffin.co.uk.www.puffin.co.uk

interviews.e-mailupdates.bookinfo.competitions.news

www.puffin.co.uk

games.sneakpreviews.adventure.bestsellers.fun

www.puffin.co.uk.www.puffin.co.uk.www.puffin.co.uk

bookinfo.competitions.news.games.sneakpreviews

www.puffin.co.uk.www.puffin.co.uk.www.puffin.co.uk

adventure.bestsellers.fun.coollinks.freestuff

www.puffin.co.uk.www.puffin.co.uk.www.puffin.co.uk

explore.yourshout.awards.toptips.authorinfo

www.puffin.co.uk.www.puffin.co.uk.www.puffin.co.uk

greatbooks.greatbooks.greatbooks.greatbooks

www.puffin.co.uk.www.puffin.co.uk.www.puffin.co.uk

reviews.poems.jokes.authorevents.audioclips

www.puffin.co.uk.www.puffin.co.uk.www.puffin.co.uk

Read more in Puffin

For complete information about books available from Puffin – and Penguin – and how to order them, contact us at the appropriate address below. Please note that for copyright reasons the selection of books varies from country to country.

www.puffin.co.uk

In the United Kingdom: Please write to Dept EP, Penguin Books Ltd,
Bath Road, Harmondsworth, West Drayton, Middlesex UB7 ODA

In the United States: Please write to Penguin Putnam Inc., P.O. Box 12289,
Dept B, Newark, New Jersey 07101–5289 or call 1–800–788–6262

In Canada: Please write to Penguin Books Canada Ltd,
10 Alcorn Avenue, Suite 300, Toronto, Ontario M4V 3B2

In Australia: Please write to Penguin Books Australia Ltd,
P.O. Box 257, Ringwood, Victoria 3134

In New Zealand: Please write to Penguin Books (NZ) Ltd,
Private Bag 102902, North Shore Mail Centre, Auckland 10

In India: Please write to Penguin Books India Pvt Ltd,
11 Panscheel Shopping Centre, Panscheel Park, New Delhi 110 017

In the Netherlands: Please write to Penguin Books Netherlands bv,
Postbus 3507, NL–1001 AH Amsterdam

In Germany: Please write to Penguin Books Deutschland GmbH,
Metzlerstrasse 26, 60594 Frankfurt am Main

In Spain: Please write to Penguin Books S. A., Bravo Murillo 19,
1° B, 28015 Madrid

In Italy: Please write to Penguin Italia s.r.l.,
Via Felice Casati 20, I–20124 Milano

In France: Please write to Penguin France S. A.,
17 rue Lejeune, F–31000 Toulouse

In Japan: Please write to Penguin Books Japan, Ishikiribashi Building,
2–5–4, Suido, Bunkyo-ku, Tokyo 112

In South Africa: Please write to Longman Penguin Southern Africa (Pty) Ltd,
Private Bag X08, Bertsham 2013